Alex Kaufman

Time Flies

A Collection of Short Stories

Time Flies

Copyright © 2014 by Alex Kaufman

ISBN-10: 0692386408
ISBN-13: 978-0-692-38640-8
Library of Congress Control Number: 2014919194

Intervale Publishing, New York, NY

Time Flies

The Muse Made Me Do It

Yes, the muse made me do it. It just hit me one day and led me to pick up a few snapshots from an active life. What might be a bit unusual about it is that this life is played in different arenas, seemingly unconnected. It appears so only because we live in a world of specialties. College, that last preparatory pit stop before entering the big race, emphasizes majoring in a trade or discipline that will enable the practitioner to pay his mortgage on time. Some go to acquire more specialized expertise, such as law, medicine and the sciences. High-tech and finance may of course turn the tables on any traditional projections of success.

I just couldn't do it. By instinct and nature, I assume, I pursued things that were of interest to me. Then, I woke up one early morning shortly after midnight, and asked myself whether I can afford this? No, was the short version answer. So you are going to keep at it? Yes, was another short version answer. I just could not do otherwise. I was committed to follow my interests, my insatiable curiosity and delve into things that I felt I could master, eventually control and lead. I am a lousy follower and joiner. It never worked for me.

The following snapshots may give the impression of a Jack of All Trades. I really hate this quote, it is so old establishment, narrow and one can sense the flutter of unease, derision, and yes fright of something that is not a run of the mill pattern that everybody does. It makes people uncomfortable, especially the humorless masses among the work force, management and bureaucracies.

I never considered myself a Jack of All Trades. I am not. My trade is ideas, a universal commodity to me, which I apply to many parts and segments of business. Their purpose is to improve upon the existing and to innovate. How to inject excitements into the daily trudge and how to elicit sounds, not from the latest, ever improving apps, but rather from the Oh's and Ah's emanating from the mouths of people.

As I look around observing, I still do not see one item, object or situation, be it in life experience, art, design, architecture, planning, marketing, building shelters, politics, military and education endeavors, that could not use a dash of a new idea and the introduction of some originality. In my sandbox, common sense rules and comes wrapped in a healthy sense of humor. It is the raw material, the putty to build with and which holds everything together. Otherwise, the redundant things we do will fade and be plain boring.

The fields of my activity were all related in some fashion to my core discipline of design, and knowledge of construction, tied to various forms and applications. I designed exhibitions and museums and used some of the portable technologies to design a method for mass, rapidly-installed housing for overseas venues. I applied my knowledge of containerization to the transport of goods to enable the cost effective delivery of such houses. I was working extensively in the international arena through a company I founded that provided promotional projects to many international airlines and shipping companies and national tourism and trade ministries. The need to house my facilities and offices in my New York City base required the purchase of buildings, which in turn got me into the business of real estate, which I then expanded further. My affinity for the dynamics of business and finance, my fascination with people, and my marveling to no end at human nature, a kaleidoscope of ever-changing images, fascinating, aggravating and always unexpected, joined with my cultural activities, provided me with a rich playing field. In time, I was asked to lend consulting services to mainly international projects providing my sizable international experience to corporations. I was well paid but found that many times people do not want to be told the truth and most hate or have great trepidation of change.

My ability to generate workable, feasible and implementable ideas that work and show targeted results came in tandem with a commodity, call it 'Siamese Twins' if you will, namely humor. But, it was never for the sake of being funny. It was for loosening things up, for drawing attention, for making something memorable in a pleasant way and to prick pomposity, chafe self-importance and get down to business without unnecessary accoutrements.

Traveling nowadays, at home and overseas, I am struck by a new phenomenon - the exposure of naked napes when not covered by long hair fashions. It is hard to look people in the eye now. No one looks up anymore. All look down, glued to their smart phones and exposing the backs of their necks. Some Ermenegildo Zegna or a Ralph Lauren will surely come up with some fashion item to fit this baring nape phenomena. The entire universe is absorbed in furiously digitizing at high speed as fast as their fingers can flex. Millions and billions of people are engaged in it with no age limit. I see this formation of a tight knit global community of smart phone holders. No politician or leader or king could achieve this. The smart phone did. Has it outsmarted us? Phone holders without borders. An amazing thing.

So here I am trying to tell a few little adventures that occurred to me while traipsing through this planet. It's a pretty good planet actually, as planets go. Then again, there is not much of an alternative, that's the one we got. Why tell it now? I said it at the outset - the Muse made me do it.

Alex Kaufman, New York, NY

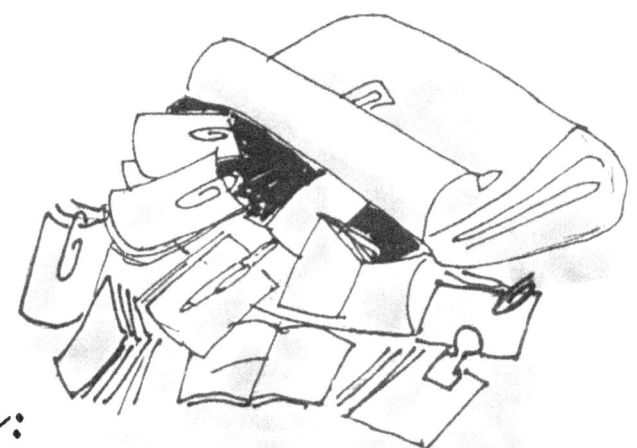

Contents:

A Collection of Short Stories

Stepping into
Grandpa's Footsteps

Grandfather arrived from Europe in 1881. He went through New York without stopping, straight down to Wilmington, Delaware. Why to Wilmington when most others stayed in New York? I can only assume that he must have had a cousin there. The history of immigration is anchored in cousins. Immigrants from Europe before the turn of the century and after, all went to where a cousin had preceded them, sort of prepared the ground and knew his way around and who had not been eaten by the natives or disappeared in some mysterious way. That's where they usually settled.

Grandfather left Ulanov, his village in south-central Poland, which at that time was under the Austro-Hungarians, as a sixteen year old. His objective was America and he was determined to get there. He had no money, figuring to make some on the way. He walked south, crossed the Carpathian Mountains, and came down to Hungary proper. Passing peasant villages and small towns, he asked for work. At an estate with a large herd of horses, the chief caretaker wanted them ferried to a town on the Austrian border. The job required accomplished horsemanship in order to gallop the horses across the plains. Although never having ridden a horse, he hired on. At home, his mother had had a horse, blind in one eye, that was hitched to a milk wagon. No one ever rode him for fear he might collapse.

Halfway to his destination and after a fortnight of riding, although chafed and scabbed and black and blue all over, he became a competent rider after a history of falls. He delivered his charges to a horse trader at a market place at the border. He now had his steerage money. Only later did he find out that the horses he had ferried were stolen. In the process however, he had become a rider who knew his horses. He figured that it might stand him in good stead in America, the land of the cowboys. He promptly proceeded to the port of LeHavre on the French Atlantic coast to board the first available ship to the New World.

***

After about ten years in Wilmington, working in general stores, construction and haulage and at the ripe age of twenty-six, he decided to return to Europe to find a wife, something that had eluded him in Delaware. Rather than go all the way back to his village in the east, another cousin living in Germany persuaded him to stay in the southern city of Mannheim and settle there. And settle he did, siring over sixteen offspring, most born before the First World War, from two wives. His first wife and two daughters perished in the typhoid epidemic that swept Germany during World War I.

He established a thriving business and his kids, over time, all emigrated to America or to British-Mandated Palestine. He and grandmother left again for America on the day WWII broke out on September 1, 1939. He, of course, returned to 'his' state Delaware and to Wilmington, which had grown a bit but had not changed too radically from the Wilmington he remembered.

He was always my hero. He was a character. A risk taker, he had a glint in his eye and a swagger in his step and was always poised and ready for the next 'never done before' thing. We used to take walks when I was a four-and-a-half year-old toddler. A bit later we used to go to the main railroad station where I could see the big locomotives close up. I liked to look at trains, and I liked their hissing and puffing. Afterwards, we used to retire to the cavernous station restaurant and bar. He would sit me on a chair next to him and would let me sip from his beer stein. I liked that a lot. Boy that was really good.

Grandpa also loved mechanical gadgets. One day he bought manual hair clippers, the kind barbers used.

"Can I try it out on your head, Alex?" he asked me.

"Of course, Grandpa," I eagerly answered, wanting to be part of the adventure. So he tried it. Doing it even and straight was the art of the barbers, it seemed, but he had a hard time with it. He went ever higher on the back of my head.

Eventually he turned me around and said, "It'll never come out straight and I do not like to leave it uneven. Why don't I cut off everything and then it'll grow back even? Do you mind?"

"No, no I don't mind. Go ahead, Opa."

He kissed me on my head and then chopped off the rest of the hair.

When I got off his chair and glanced at the mirror on the commode in the living room, for a second I thought that my head, from a certain angle, looked a bit like my rear end. I told him that, and he assured me that there was no room for concern.

My mother at first did not recognize me. Looking again, she fainted. When she came to, she screamed at him. "What did you do to my son!?"

To alleviate the damage, grandfather went out and bought a big straw-hat that covered my ears.

He was my role model, although I had no particular role in mind, I wanted to model after. I just wanted to be like him.

I arrived in America seventy-one years later, also by sea, on the Queen Elizabeth of all ships, and on a scorching July day in 1954. I was going to rush to Wilmington to see him, but he had passed away two years earlier, followed shortly by Grandma.

Tom, an old acquaintance, let me use his apartment while he was away for the summer. It was in a working class neighborhood at that time, on the Upper East Side of New York, on Seventy-Fifth Street and Third Avenue, in a five-story walk-up. The elevated subway ran along Third Avenue and made an unholy racket, with the buildings shaking every time it went by.

My money was rapidly running out and I needed a job. I was ready to go to work that very afternoon.

While I was contemplating my next steps, the phone rang.

I grabbed a pen and a piece of paper, ready for a message for Tom.

"It's Joyce, from L.A., the actress," she reminded Tom, who was not there. "Who are you?" she demanded to know.

"The butler," I replied.

"I'm coming up, I'm here for a day and I need a place to crash."

"OK," I said, having no idea what she meant by that 'crash,' or did she say trash? Or cash? My English was dictionary English and I was not yet familiar with the local slang and idioms. I was at a loss. I looked it up in the dictionary and all I found were allusions to catastrophes. I became real curious. What is she going to do to this place? I pondered. I looked around and concluded that anything that would be done to the place could only be considered an improvement. So why not?

She climbed up all five floors, stopping at the door, huffing, puffing, and trying to catch her breath. She threw her suitcase ahead of her through the door and had barely made it in before she slumped down on the floor, and sprawled out flat, her arms outstretched, breathing heavily with her suitcases on top of her, bobbing up and down. I offered her water and it took her a while to come to. After a time, she slowly got up and looked around. Joyce was not fashionably skinny, yet she was attractive and more in the 'saftig' mode.

"Some butler you are," she said, as she got up from the floor, "…you don't look like a butler."

"What's a butler look like?" I kept this idiotic conversation going.

"I knew that Tom, that cheapskate, could not afford a butler," she said. Pretty perceptive woman, this one, I figured.

"Did Tom know that you were coming?"

"How could he know? I did not know myself that I was coming until Bill called me last night."

Now I was really in the picture. But at least the cast of characters was growing. I was finally getting to know some people in America.

"Who's Bill?" I tried.

"Bill Tuttle," she said and disappeared in the bathroom. "The make-up guy," she called out from behind the closed door.

"Of course," I slapped my forehead, Bill Tuttle, who else? Ask a stupid question.

We went down to get a ninety-nine cent meal at a Chinese place. Now there were two of us with no money and there was nothing to pool. The pool was dry. So we sat and had a lengthy dinner. It was two dollars and fifty cents for the both of us, with the tip, so why were they rushing us? The Chinese wanted to close the store for the night, but Joyce was now waking up and told me all about her career and Bill Tuttle.

Bill was William Tuttle, the famous Hollywood make-up man who dabbled as a director of summer stock productions. His name appeared on hundreds of film credits, too numerous to mention. He was in great demand and his standing in Hollywood gave him the ability to draw stars to his productions. Tuttle had chosen Joyce for his cast. He was producing and directing two plays in Wilmington, Delaware. And that was where she was going to tomorrow morning.

"What?" I jumped out of my seat. "Wilmington, Delaware? You are going to Wilmington? That's where my whole family is from; my grandfather went there from Europe in the last century and returned before the outbreak of the first war. He is buried in Wilmington and so is my grandmother. I have three uncles there and a whole slew of cousins and other relatives. The town is full of them." Joyce's eyes lit up.

"About how many relatives you got there, would you say? Just give me a guess. A hundred? More? They have friends, don't they?"

Suddenly it hit me that Joyce was filling up theater seats. More power to her. That's America, no small talk about culture and message and all that crap. Simple and direct: how many bodies can we conjure up to fill the theater?

Joyce now waded full–time into the planning mode. She was totally recovered from her afternoon climb. Like it never happened, or maybe it was the MSG in the roast pork fried rice? Whether it was or not, the girl was cooking, big time.

"Listen," she said, "...you just got in from Europe. Do you know what plays we are doing? One is Toulouse Lautrec with the 'Moulin Rouge' thing; the other is 'Boy Meets Girl.' You were in Paris, you are an artist, you know the scene and you are perfect for the job. We will need scenery and backgrounds. I'll tell Bill to send you a bus ticket. You will have room and board and probably get paid. And what the hell are you going to do here in the summer anyway?"

I paid special attention to the word probably she so casually inserted. But I liked the idea. The free bus ticket was a factor, too. And I had to visit the relatives sooner or later and maybe that probably would turn into a definitely. Who could tell? And maybe this Joyce, this high-voltage girl, could get me a job somewhere later. I was faced with a basket full of opportunities and I decided to take them all.

The morning after her departure, the phone rang again. Joyce was true to her word. "Bill is enthused about your coming," Joyce pronounced from Wilmington. She had told him all about her find and they were all awaiting my arrival, especially Diane who was eager to meet this European artist. Diane, turned out, was Diane Barrymore. Well, I was called names before, but never a European Artist. What the heck, I thought - at least I can flaunt my accented English.

We fixed a date for my trip and my ETA in Wilmington. Joyce was going to pick me up at the Trailways Bus Station, as indeed she did. In close to three hours the bus shot down the newly opened New Jersey

Turnpike, crossed the Delaware Memorial Bridge and voila, I was in Wilmington. It reminded me of the town of Hadera in Israel, but with less sand. But not bad.

Joyce took me in tow; we drove through the main street of the town and then swung into the parking lot of the local movie theater. In the rear of the theater, spread out on a vacant lot, were four large live-in trailers and two trucks, loaded with scenery, panels, canvas covered frames and electrical equipment. Inside, the movie screen was removed and at that moment it became a legitimate stage theater for the next four weeks.

Joyce dragged me from trailer to trailer and introduced me to all the players, stage hands, electricians, hangers-on and all kinds of people running around in their underwear trying to look important. Then we went to see Diane. She had a trailer all to herself. As we entered, she was sprawled on her bed, which took up the major portion of the trailer, clad in a silk robe with one cigarette in her mouth and one in her hand on a silver holder and a full ashtray next to her. A headband, that looked like a tiara with a stone and a feather in the middle, held her unruly hair in place.

"Come here, let me look at you," she growled.

"Don't get any closer," Joyce hissed into my ear as I was advancing. I stopped halfway.

"Are you going to make me a nice background? Don't make it dark, it gets too harsh when the light hits me. Make it rosy like. Will you do this, sweetheart? Ooooh, I like this kid," she cooed. And I had not even said a word yet.

There was a little two-tier tea table next to her bed filled with liquor bottles. I liked the place. It was messy, but felt homey. Life, Colliers, Vogue – every magazine around was there, plastering the floor. This woman sure was a reader, I thought. Cornflake boxes were interspersed with publicity pictures of her in various films. I liked her. She seemed to be a nice person, when people did not confuse her. She had a giant legacy to protect, yet she was unpretentious and looked like she was in my corner, so long as I did not make the background dark.

Then we hung out on the steps of another trailer with a bunch of people. Most were dancers, very skinny customers, walking around in skimpy clothes or none at all, but always with woolen leggings, constantly making bends, stretching, and drinking juice till about five in the afternoon, when they switched to more potent libations.

"You came on the new Turnpike, how was it? Was it fast?" they asked in wonderment.

"What is a Turnpike? I mean is this what it's called?" They all thought this to be very funny. I was serious.

I did not know that the Turnpike had just opened and that I had the privilege to be among its first users and I also did not know that a straight paved road without turns is called a Turnpike. We kept talking about the adventures and advantages of riding a bus down the new New Jersey Turnpike.

Bill had come back from wherever he had been. He was a very, very nice gentleman. He was considerate, fair, polite, accommodating, a prince. He took a liking to me right away and told me that he trusted me with the whole shebang. He was of compact build, well-groomed and projected professionalism and competence. In short, he knew what he was doing. For me, it was back to dictionary searching for this shebang I had been entrusted with.

It started to dawn on me that this was a mutual assistance society deal. The thought crept into my mind that they needed me as much as I needed them. Maybe not the same. Maybe I was a bit ahead of this game, but it would be prudent for me to play along, no matter what the rewards were going to be. I also realized, that to my surprise, I had almost become the center cog in this enterprise, and I had not even started yet.

Bill told me that he was leaving for New York to talk to some Angels. He suggested that I get started in the meantime. He reminded me again of his full trust in my work and that I was free to do what I wanted so long as the paint lasted. I guess there was no money to buy more paint. Being a take-charge type, I could not have asked for better. Obviously, he did not know that I had no clue what to do and how to start his shebang.

"In five days we open," he revealed to me. I was naturally included in the we as if I had been with them my entire life. So I should have plenty of time to do the backgrounds for Moulin Rouge and the Toulouse Lautrec vignettes, about six changeovers.

"Then, the following week, we'll do Boy Meets Girl," he assured me. I wasn't crazy about the title and suggested to Bill that he change it. He just smiled benevolently and explained that it would raise great objections, what with Adele and Samuel Spivak, the authors, and Clifton Fadiman who was also involved with the movie. Then he mentioned copyright laws and a host of other things, ending by saying that my suggestion had merit and should be discussed further. Later when I understood a bit more about the American theater, I wondered how Bill was not ever hijacked into the Diplomatic Corps.

A pick-up truck delivered the paints in five gallon cans along with a whole package of brushes, the hard yellow tipped ones, so well-suited for painting on canvas.

The canvas was being stretched at the back of the stage and I went to work. I decided to use a light type of art, a bit in the vein of Dufy. There was the Mill on the Pigalle, the inside of the dance hall, an outdoor café scene with the round free-standing billboard kiosk, a night scene (sorry Diane) of the Eiffel Tower with lots of little lights, an art-noveau Metro entrance sign and a flower cart against a background of people with umbrellas.

The scenery was huge, the length and the height of the entire stage. Gigantic. I went up the ladder, down the ladder, running to the last row of the theater, gauging scale, observing proportions, back up the ladder, then repeating the whole thing over and over again. It was a lot of work and I used a lot of paint. I had two full-time helpers in addition to whoever came by. I drew the outline and my helpers and onlookers did the 'fillings.'

When Bill returned from the Angels, which at first I thought he referred to a religious retreat until it was explained to me, he just stood there at the far end of the theater, clasping his hands on his stomach, nodding his head with a satisfying smile on his face.

"I knew it, I told you so," he exclaimed to his ensemble that crowded around him. "I knew it, this kid is good! Joyce! Where are you? Kudos to you."

"You did dark scenery," Diane, who appeared from nowhere, spotted me at the other end and wagged her finger and chided me, when the Eiffel Tower scene came on.

"But it's a night scene, Diane."

"Don't have to be dark."

"Leave him alone Diane. Dark blue will bring out your colors, you'll see," Bill assuaged her.

Bill was really elated. "Do we have enough paint for Boy Meets Girl?" he inquired.

"We'll need some more. But we have only three changeovers for that play. We'll need greens, blues and yellows and I'll stretch it."

"That's a relief, thank you. You know your name is on the program," Bill told me.

Wow, I hadn't made a penny yet, but I had gotten my name in print.

***

When I had a minute to spare it occurred to me that my relatives lived here, so I called my aunt, my mother's sister.

"Where are you? Are you in America?" came the frantic question.

"Yes, I am."

"When did you land? Are you in New York? In Brooklyn? Where?"

"I landed last week in New York." My aunt equated New York with Brooklyn, where she had once lived.

"When will you come to Wilmington?"

"I am in Wilmington!"

"In Wilmington?" came back a gasping answer.

"Yeah, and I am inviting you to the theater, I'll get free tickets for everybody, tell the others."

"What? What? What theater? What tickets? Where do you live?"

After I gave her the general outline of my doings, there was silence on the line, then the attack resumed.

"You mean you live with the gypsies? In a parking lot? Braverman!" She called out to her eighth husband. I guess she called them by their last names to avoid confusion and keep them all in proper order. "Come here, did you hear this? My nephew, Toni's son lives with the gypsies in the parking lot of the movie house. Who do you still know in the Police Department? Is Jimmy still there?"

Then turning back to me, she said, "When are you coming over?"

"As soon as I am finished with my work." I had now started hatching a plot on how to get out of it.

At the end I went to see them. I brought them tickets. They came reluctantly to the shows. They had never been to a theater. This explained part of their reticence. The other was the culture clash and the wondering where I would end up and that they might have to take care of me, pull me out of some gutter and how much all this would set them back.

The performances were a success as far as Wilmington was concerned. Bill's productions clicked with the local audience and Diane Barrymore was not called a star for nothing and she really looked good in Paris at night, especially against the dark Eiffel Tower scenery. The Can-Can dancers were great and the applause reverberated onto Main Street. I was fed and housed and was paid with compliments, theater tickets, and some pocket money. Then I dug out my Trailways bus ticket, hopped the bus north and landed in New York for the second time.

***

The glamour days of summer cavorting with Hollywood stars over, I was back in New York and burying my nose in the New York Times Want Ads. I needed a job for the money, but still gravitated towards ad sections headlined ARTIST. I did not realize the width and breadth of this term. Then again, I was entering my second month in the country and the question arose as to what to do and where to do it. People migrate all the time following the job venues. Since I did not have a job, the venue was of my making. Do I stay in the East, do I go to the West, as Bill Tuttle suggested, or do I go camping out in the middle? Every morning I got up excited, so many things could happen, it was like I was sitting in the middle of a giant supermarket with every item within reach. Yes it was, but not exactly. By ten o'clock in the morning my state of excitement would dim a bit and impatience would set in. 'I've got to move forward, this is taking too long,' my mind was repeating endlessly. And I needed money and could not detect the well I could bring it up from.

No one would hire without experience, but how does one gain experience without being hired? Some of the individuals who interviewed me I would not have hired as gofers in my company, if I had one. Yet they sat on the right side of the desk where their pay envelope was delivered every Friday.

I was in a Catch 22. I had practically no contacts, no school friends to call on. So I circulated. By day I made as many appointments as I could muster, no matter whether they were relevant or irrelevant to my specific task and, at night, I tried to get invited to parties and talk people up. It occurred to me then that, when mentioning maladies that seem to befall Americans, such as heart attacks, the fight for weight loss and the fight against hair loss, they forgot to include memory loss. You meet a guy one day, warm and effusive, next day he was like in a coma, he did not recall your name, or what he had said, let alone had promised.

'Well, it isn't the end of the world,' I thought, '...there are lots of doors and all I have to do is find one that opens.' What was irksome was that I could do a lot of things better, more imaginatively, employ common sense and deliver a higher quality and I could make them money. In the process of visiting all these companies, big and small and the medium ones in-between, I could then and there suggest improvements to their operations. I told this to some of the managers who interviewed me, but I felt it did not sit too well with them. To one who asked me how far I wanted to go in their company, I told him - after I was convinced that I would not be doing business with this guy - that for starters I'd concentrate on getting his job, president, a little later.

Somewhere however, it left an impression. I was interviewed by a very prominent national food company's marketing department. I must have scared its manager, who wanted the chairman of the company to hear my ideas about the introduction of a new product they were about to launch. It was a case where he would have wanted to own the idea but was afraid to stick his neck out, needing the assurance of a nod from higher up, then he'd go all the way and steal the idea. On the way upstairs, to the very top floor, he nervously kept telling me what to say. "I thought you bring me up here because you wanted the chairman to hear what I have to say?" I tried to preempt him.

We stepped off the elevator and entered the holy sanctum of the chairman. Interestingly, all these beautiful well-coifed, long-legged blonde secretaries I had expected were not to be found there. Instead, there was a group of older ladies, conservatively dressed, traditionally-coifed in grey, wearing sensible shoes, bespectacled and with knowing miens and exuding competence.

First question to me out of the chairman's mouth was "...and what is your experience with food?" I expected it, and I decided to tell the truth.

"Sir, for the past thirty seven years I was eating."

Now the chairman looked up. The room was silent for a few minutes. He got up, walked around me, tapped me on the shoulder and said, "…from the looks of it, your choice of food seems to have been excellent."

His underlings did not know what to say. I didn't get a job, but I felt good on the way out. I left an impression which came back to me years later, when I ran my own company and got their firm as a client. I was told that the chairman remembered me when he was asked his approval to award me the project. I was told that over the years, he had repeated my interview with him to his cronies and partners.

It's funny. When you walk in and know that you have nothing to lose, you feel free, trim, unburdened. There is nothing to calculate until one is advanced to a position where one would have something to lose. Then I'd start calculating my thoughts, my words and my behavior.

I gave the New York Times one more week. My response to an ad brought me to one Joe Appelbaum in a palatial apartment on a high floor in a building on Central Park West across the street from the Hayden Planetarium. His very blond wife Shirley opened the door.

I felt that I had seen this whole setting before, including the wife in her plastic, see-through shoes, displaying every little toe. The high-ceilinged rooms, the white furniture, the chandeliers. Then it came to me, I had seen this in the movies, the black and white ones of those days. Joe came ambling in to greet me. He was a tall, lanky man and I had the impression that he was the kind of guy who could not hurt a fly - in short, a good guy. And so he turned out to be.

He explained to me that he had a new business and needed someone to design the products for it. I was listening and had no clue what he was talking about. We moved over to the next room where he pulled out a pile of ceramic tiles, the type that are being used on kitchen and on bathroom walls.

"These are Greeting Tiles," he announced somberly. "They come in a gift box and are sold in souvenir shops. Got it?"

I was at a loss on how to react, but I kept the conversation going. I asked him what was on my mind from the moment I entered his apartment:

"Joe, was your apartment ever used for a movie set?"

Now Joe was flabbergasted. But he answered "No," and went back to his spiel about the tiles.

What Joe did was to print line drawings of famous American tourist sites and landmarks - such as Mount Rushmore, The Old Man of the Mountain, the Capitol, the Golden Gate Bridge, the Statue of Liberty and so on. He would then sell these tiles to national distributors who in turn would place them in the gift shops at these sites. The idea was that I would do the outline of the scene and then divide it into fields and put numbers on them, and these numbers would correlate with colors. My mind went numb just to listen to it. But I needed the money. Thus, the Greeting Tile, a mini paint-by-number set, would include a set of paint tubes and a brush. The whole thing was attractively packaged for sale at the various landmark gift shops. To me, this whole thing was crazy. The most boring thing I had come across so far. Joe noticed my hesitation and kept raising the ante. All of a sudden the money was not too bad, so I agreed. 'I'll do it for a while, at least I will make some money,' I thought. Above all, I needed the money.

Next day, Joe picked me up in his white Cadillac convertible with red upholstery and we went to the factory in Brooklyn. The building was located in Red Hook, directly across the street from the docks. There was nothing there. Joe's so-called factory was a floor in a semi-abandoned factory building that had one or two other tenants. Two black, man-eating Rottweiler dogs patrolled the yard. The floor was clean and heated. I got a big office with a view of New York Harbor and the Statue of Liberty practically looking at me. Now who could beat that?

Joe farmed out the silk-screen printing of the tiles and the packaging. I also found out that I was the only full time employee, although a bookkeeper was hovering around most of the time.

I turned out the line drawings and put little numbers in them and at the same time, I started to make contacts with international airline advertising and public relations managers for design work. So far I had almost half a dozen airlines willing to consider my services for the exhibition design, marketing and interiors for their terminals. However, until these projects materialized I had to see some money. I used my lunchtime breaks to conduct my airlines business affairs. Down on the corner was a bar. The street was totally deserted except for the occasional passing by of one of the giant forklifts from the docks to the bar. On the other opposite corner was a combination luncheonette-candy store and bookie-joint. The entrance was on the corner. As one entered, on the right, was a long counter almost the length of the store with nogahyde-covered swivel stools. On the left were a number of booths that I had never seen unoccupied at all the entire time I went there. At the far end were two telephone booths, leaning against the toilets. It seemed that people lived in these booths. They went in, yet no one ever came out. The whole thing was sitting on a cracked linoleum-covered floor with some of the original wooden floor planks showing through. The owner of that dive was the heavy-set but agile Dante.

This dive though, was my day off-site office. I used to settle into one of the phone booths to the chagrin of the bookies who regarded me as their competitor, and made my solicitation calls to the other side of the river, to other clients and to my suppliers, lining up appointments in Manhattan. I befriended Dante - his sandwiches were great and affordable and I made my first acquaintance with heroes, the kind you can eat.

Dante did not mind that I occupied the phone booth for almost an hour every day. He preferred it over the sleaze balls as he called them, in there. It was also safer when the cops came by. The bookies had a thriving business, and the booths were constantly busy. Traffic materialized from nowhere. Every second people walked in and out. The door could have been used as a hinge-tester. Open - shut, open - shut. It went on like this all day. So many people and yet the street was totally deserted, how could this be? It couldn't and I never found the true answer.

I drew a portrait of Dante holding a giant hero on his arms, parallel with his mustache, two big horizontal lines and his bushy eyebrows, and always in his dirty T-shirt whose original color was impossible to determine. He wore it summer and winter, he may have slept in it too, and he was always yelling and always there. He would change my dollars into nickels for the phone. I was his kid.

Many times during lunchtime, a Cadillac, followed by two or three other cars would pull up at the corner and out would come a guy with blond hair, accompanied by a phalanx of people who kept emerging from the other cars. Dante would give the blond guy a big hello and within seconds, heaps of steaming plates would appear in front of the guy and his entourage. They all drank beer, except for the blond guy, who drank coke. They did a lot of talking with their hands, not conversational talk, rather a pushing kind of talk, a very physical talk. To get someone's attention and be heard, they would push in a manner that would knock an unsuspecting bystander right off his stool. Then there would start the slapping on the back barrages. I figured it must take some resiliency and training to get used to it, let alone bear it.

One day, as I sat at the counter eating my hero, they surrounded me and kept talking and slapping 'through' me and around me. I wanted to move a bit down so as to give them freedom of movement and a more contiguous space.

"Naaaa…. no need kid, stay. What's your name?"

I told them.

"I'm Joey Gallo," volunteered the blond guy.

"You make wine Joey?" I asked innocently wanting to be social and remembering that I saw the name on bottles somewhere.

"What? Ha ha-ha…." Joey cracked up. And when Joey cracked up, his entire gang cracked up with him. Knees were slapped, people bent over backwards, staggering and bumping into furniture and fixtures. When he gained his second wind Joey yelled in ecstasy amid coughing attacks, "You're OK, this kid is a pistol - making wine… hahaha… yuch… hahaha, get a load of that…." Resuming a second breathless attack he called out, "I am going to have an accident…." and with that he disappeared behind the phone booths.

I looked at Dante. Dante busied himself with the coffeemaker. I did not get it.

"And what do you do, kid? Need a job?" Joey, now relieved, asked me.

"No, thank you, I've got a job," I said with a smile.

"What kind of a job? You're smart, what are you an Irish Mick or a Jew boy?"

"Jewish smart, Joey. My boss is also a Joe."

"Holy mother, this kid is a comedian, he's a riot, somebody help me." And gasping for air again, "What kind of work you do?"

"Greeting Tiles, paint by number…."

At that Joey cracked up again. Now he was literally on the floor. There was a danger that the whole joint was going to get demolished by his crack-ups. I thought he might choke. Tears were streaming down his face, he lost his aviator sunglasses, his face was crimson and he was beside himself.

"You're doing numbers? With Greeting Cards?"

I guess one hears what one wants to hear. Dante came to my rescue to straighten out matters. But, from that day on, every time Joey saw me, I rated one of his slaps of approval, the ones you could die from. His gang wanted to award me their approval too, but I succeeded in dissuading them from it, assuring them that the boss's approval sufficed.

"He keeps a lion in his basement," Dante told me about Joey Gallo.

"Oh," I said, "…where I came from they kept lions in regular rooms in a house and sometimes they would come out and sit on the terrace." I was thinking of the very beginning of the Tel Aviv zoo when it was located in a house on Hayarkon Street.

"What racket were they in?" Dante asked, deeply impressed.

"The zoo racket," I said, always telling the truth.

Years later, Joey was shucking his last oyster one early morning at Umberto's on Mulberry Street in Little Italy when he was gunned down on his stool by the competition. He should have stuck to Dante's. It was a much safer place. I found out more about him and his Mafia faction.

The lion was his collection agent. Clients who were in arrears were brought down to his basement and the lion would provide the incentive for a rapid payment schedule. When The Gang Who Could Not Shoot Straight by Jimmy Breslin was published, I could almost make out the players in the drama. I met them for lunch daily in Red Hook. They did not strike me as cerebral giants. Joey had a very crazy kind look in his eyes. But I did not know then what important work they were engaged in.

I liked Red Hook despite the fact that whenever I mentioned it to anyone and the fact that I worked there, people were either shocked or stricken with pity. In parting I felt, they behaved as if saying a final goodbye to me. They were curious, in the sense of "What are you really doing there and stop these stories about the stupid greeting tiles, come up with a better cover." Others again regarded me with a degree of guarded respect due to the mysterious and romantic unknown I was probably engaged in.

The neighborhood was great and the people were nice to me. The longshoremen used to sit along the fence, smoking and eating and drinking. Bums used to come along and tell tall tales. A musician would appear here and there. And a New York was revealed to me that I was sure few people saw or knew. I got off daily at the Joralemon subway stop, walked through Brooklyn Heights and down Atlantic Avenue under the BQE / Gowanus to 55 Ferris Street in Red Hook. There was always something interesting to observe.

Dante and his surroundings were Italian, family-oriented people. I liked them. There were kids and old people and the view was spectacular. The Statue of Liberty could be seen pretty close by, when the containers on the docks were not piled too high. It was a sort of end-of-the-line neighborhood. It seemed like the city had forgotten about it. No police ever came there, no inspectors, no street cleaners, no one. It was a self-governing entity and there was a hierarchy that no one challenged.

I was recognized in the neighborhood and Dante assured everybody that I was trustworthy and was only passing through. Everyone seemed to know me and said hello. It was like in a small village. When Joe Appelbaum had qualms one day about leaving me neglected and alone, a new immigrant in a strange place, I took him for coffee at Dante's and introduced him to everybody I knew and to the ones I did not know. Even the bookies took time off to shake his hand after Dante seized them with a fierce look. Joe sat there with his mouth agape; he had to call his blond Shirley to tell her that he is with the refugee kid, who is almost the mayor of the neighborhood. To Joe anyone who came through Europe was a refugee. As we rode back, he shook his head all the way to Manhattan, full of amazement of my local popularity.

I always thought that that section of Red Hook would make a beautiful park on the water. Dante and his customers got excited about the idea. They badly needed some leadership. I received hints but I was finally leaving Red Hook behind for good. I'd come to visit, I promised. In a way I missed it all a little.

From Red Hook my phone calls and burgeoning career took me to another part of the city, or for a better description to another planet. My next theater of operation called on my cartooning skills and centered around Madison Avenue and Fifty-Seventh Street. When I first arrived Tom took me to Irving Trust's bank branch on Fifty-Seventh and Madison, giving me five hundred dollars to open an account.

"I do not want this fortune of money and why do I have to open an account?" I objected.

"Yes you do," he replied, "You need it for credit reference, to write checks. You pay it back to me and do not worry, it'll cost you."

"This is what I am afraid of," I retorted while still trying to wiggle out of it.

Tom Friedman was like Swiss cheese. He had lots of holes, but between the holes was a lot of good stuff. The five hundred dollars was easily repaid because I never touched it. But the interest, oh the interest, that went on forever.

Diagonally across the street from the bank on Fifty-Seventh Street was a beautiful, small building squeezed between the high rises, occupied by Mr. John. That was the name of the firm, a millinery store, selling high fashion ladies hats. Presiding over the store, was, who else but Mr. John. I was to go and meet with Mr. John and design a promotional Christmas card for his store.

To meet with Mr. John one needed an appointment months in advance. Since I was not in the market for any of his exquisite hats, I was able to see him within the span of a few days of my call.

He was a chubby, immaculately dressed, manicured, coifed and polished man. He wore a vest and, in place of a tie, he had a wildly fluttering silk scarf tied to his neck. From his chest pocket, a space usually allocated to a neatly folded white handkerchief, there cascaded down another silken shawl in bright colors and polka dots. His shoes were brown and white and very pointy.

As he had just come in from the outside, he sported a fedora with the rim turned down all around. The hat was planted on his head in an askew fashion, covering one of his ears almost entirely. Mr. John did not walk; he sauntered and floated above ground. His walk was a bit reminiscent of the runway walk models do. If my recollection serves me, he ran the store with Maman, an elderly lady I saw in the store, who made for a very striking presence. Here he was, right out of central casting. Much later, he reminded me of La Cage aux Folles. He would have been absolutely perfect for it. He had a tendency to talk about three unrelated things at the same time. Since my control of English was in the developmental stage, I had to pay very close attention to what he was saying.

Suddenly, observing my total absorption to what he was mumbling, he softened. He switched from his defensive haughtiness into something closer to humanity. He was very impressed with my attentiveness.

"You are an excellent listener, ahhhh…so rare these days, ahhh." He sighed a deep complimentary sigh.

At the end we got up from the Louis XIV chairs and chaise-lounges which were the standard furnishings in the store. I drew him a card with his image on the cover and which he loved. People who heard about my doing work for Mr. John were impressed. His was a prestigious establishment. His publicity agent had him mentioned almost daily in the gossip and the society columns.

Where else, but in New York, I kept musing, can one cover the distance form Dante to Mr. John in a thirty minute subway ride.

Still no job. I was either overqualified, a left-handed compliment if there ever was one, or lacked experience, so back I went to scanning the Want Ad columns under ARTIST. With the help of an old acquaintance, I landed a job in one of the McCrory's department store branches on Queens Boulevard as a display artist, designing window displays. The manager was a very nice fellow and not used to my diligence. Monday mornings I would get a list of what to show in the windows, and then design some eye catchers for it, displaying the merchandise. One Monday, about three weeks after I was hired, I was skimming through the list I was just given and started to run down the various departments on it, ready to go and alert the different sales ladies in charge that I would need a pile of merchandise for the windows. We had twelve windows at McCrory's and we changed them as soon as we completed a cycle; we would tackle the new cycle. We had about a week in-between cycles for the preparation of the artwork eye-catcher. As I went down the handwritten list, I encountered among the pots and pans, cosmetics, blue jeans, fish in aquariums, and beachwear, what looked like the word bras. I rushed to my dictionary that I always kept in my hip pocket, and tried to find bra. Brass I found, but not bras. What on earth was it? Rather than ask the manager, I decided to ask one of the salesgirls I had become friendly with. She looked at me, covered her nose in advance of bursting out in a super giggle, ran to her colleagues and soon the whole store was cracking up. It was not a laughing matter to me; I had to do a window with it. Still not enlightened as to its meaning, I had no choice but to go to the manager.

"Brassieres, my man, what girls wear, did you ever see one?"

"Brassieres?" I said. "Why did you say bra?"

"It saves time, it's in short, that's what we call it in America."

"You can call it anything you want, but don't expect me to understand it. Trust me, even the Encyclopedia Britannica does not mention it."

"You are reading the wrong stuff, kiddo."

The job paid fifty five dollars per week. I felt stuck on Queens Boulevard, but I badly needed to replenish my empty pocket. I tried to figure out how I could make phone calls and go to interviews in Manhattan. It hit me. I went to my manager-boss again and made him an offer.

"Look, Mr. McCloskey, I will reduce your expenses, you pay me only thirty three dollars for three days at the same rate of eleven dollars a day you pay me now and I promise to do five days work in three days. How's that?"

"You can do that? You're that efficient?"

"Try me, but if you pay me twenty five dollars a day, I'll do it in two days, but like twelve hours per day? It's a good deal for you and I will get fifty dollars. Well?"

"Too rich for me, but I'll tell you what, you should get a job on Wall Street."

"They have windows there?"

"Oh do they, sometimes they jump out of them."

***

One day my roommate at the time on the upper West Side, watching my constant search for better income, suggested that I should change venues and go work for the company he was working for part time, namely the Walker Studio in the Bronx. Studio referred to photography. They sold a plan in conjunction with a diaper service, a very essential service upon arrival of a baby, way before the existence of pampers in supermarkets. The newborn was subscribed to be photographed every year for the first ten years of his life or so for free and given a large eight inch by ten inch photograph. Then one of their salesmen would call on the mother, showing twelve exposures of the little one, a whole series of pictures. Now who could refuse these sweet scenes of the little cuties? Twelve of them did not seem enough. Grandparents from both sides, uncles, aunts and sundry relatives were to be present and also ordered pictures. That was the deal and the core of the business.

To see how this worked, I went along one Friday afternoon with my roommate. As we walked in, the two year old, I believe, sat on the kitchen table, all dressed up, and drooling. He was eating an egg, stuffing it into his mouth with his hand. He was indeed a very cute kid. The minute he saw my roommate, who had a head of curly hair, the kid started to howl. To photograph a child crying was taboo, no payment for that. So my roommate tried to assuage the kid, using all his professional skills as an actor, his real job. The kid quieted down, looked at him in fascination, and called out "He's got scrambled hair!" Then he took handfuls of the eggs he was eating before and, as my friend bent down to amuse him with a facial contortion, the little one planted a load of egg smack on my roommate's head.

"Tell me is this the routine? Does this happen often?"

"There's worse, don't worry, just make faces and smile a lot."

"Beats cursing, I guess."

Two choices were offered by Walker. You could work as a salesman or as a photographer. In the latter case, the office made the appointments; all you had to do was show up at the newborn's house, empty a one hundred twenty roll of film and shoot twelve scenes. For each executed sitting you earned two dollars, and the idea was to do ten to twelve such sittings a day. At twenty bucks a day times seven days, you were getting rich; no one I knew was making one hundred forty dollars a week, that was over five hundred dollars a month. That was crazy, a gold mine, I said, "I'll do it."

The equipment was provided by Walker – tripods, background screens, lights, two cameras and films. But one needed a car. One had to get to the far reaches of Brooklyn, the Bronx and Queens, areas that even native New Yorkers had never heard of. I enlisted a relative who knew about cars. He was a noted mathematician and space scientist with a specialty on guidance systems for missiles. He was to guide me to purchase a car.

"What's your budget?" he asked.

"What's a budget?" I asked. "If you mean money, I do not have any."

"Good, so let's go to a used car dealer lot and see what they have."

We went. He researched the jumble of wires and plugs under the hoods and then pronounced a 1951 four door Dodge as suitable. It was big, sturdy and black. I bought it for sixty-five bucks. A couple of weeks later, as I stood at a light, another car rear-ended me. We settled for seventy-five dollars. My car showed no damage. The car was built like a tank. It had a two sectional windshield. Its chromed bumper was indestructible, as bumpers were supposed to be. Only the other car got damaged. Who's complaining? I had a car, I had the money and a ten dollar profit, my very first what you might call a 'profit' in these United States.

So I was driving around, stashing and unpacking the tripod, the camera bag with two loaded cameras, the two lights stands, the film bag and the folding screen, of the type that people projected movies on, into the trunk. To carry this equipment around was rather cumbersome, but it had to be done at every sitting. It was a manageable problem, what was not, was parking the car. Walker Studio was in the Bronx, but my route turned out to be mostly in Brooklyn, sometimes reaching into Queens. I could have doubled as a National Geographic explorer, or worked the streets for Google, had they been around then. Everywhere I went in Brooklyn the streets were parked solid. Some cars must have been there since WWII. They were never moved because the city never cleaned there. Double parking was a bad option, it never failed, you were either ticketed or the car you blocked needed to get out just when you arrived with all your stuff on the top floor. The Walker contractors had to pay for their fines, thus one ticket could easily wipe out your take for the day. There were some other rules – it was taboo to photograph a crying child and it had to smile and look cute, no matter how long it took to convince the little one. You had to make faces and entertain it; sometimes the faces had the opposite effect.

Depending on the baby's family background, some were all prepared and ready. We usually photographed them on a table with the screen set up behind them. Some were ready, sitting there like birthday cakes, all dressed up with the little faces barely showing through. Some were totally disheveled, with smudged faces full of food residue. We always asked to have a little container of water handy and tissues, so we could wipe them clean and we also combed their hair against their will, of course. The worst was when the little one would take a liking to us and kept climbing forward, wanting to touch and hug. In some cases, only the mother was present and had to constantly run to the kitchen on some mysterious errand, yelling "Wait! Wait!" In other instances, up to fifteen people were present, making sounds and scaring and confusing the object of this photo shoot. I needed the kid to look at the camera, but how could he if behind me, one of the uncles gesticulates with his hands and dances and the kid's eyes darted upwards, his head pointed in all directions, following his uncles' movements?

To make all this work, you had to exercise speed. Park, grab the equipment, chase up the floors, hope the kid is there, not sleeping and ready, set up the kid, watch out that he doesn't hurt you, throw things at you or drool on you and your equipment. All the while look out the window to check on the car, whether it was being ticketed, or vandalized by some of the neighborhood populace. Wrap up the sitting, rush down, and get to the next appointment, provided you can find it. Repeat this ten to twelve times and it's a piece of cake. What cake? Who had time to think of food?

The salesmen were given the contact sheets of the shoot and some larger proofs to go back with to the house where we took the pictures and start generating sales.

Now being a salesman for the initial sign-up or for peddling the pictures after the shoots were two different deals. For the initial call, it was best to show up early in the morning after the husbands left for work and the lady of the house was all by herself. It was the easiest time to talk her into it and have her sign up. After all, it was all for free, unless she then ordered extra pictures, which this was all about, so why would she refuse? There was a delicate sort of problem though – the ladies just got out of bed, sleepy heads, wearing flimsy robes and sometimes chemistry set in and people got in trouble.

It was a different story for after the shoot. Then you'd want as many relatives as possible around. The best buyers were Jews and Italians. Sales were based on the emotional impact of the pictures. No uncle or aunt, no close or distant relative would forgo a picture of the new kid, or of his images chronicling his growing up. There was excitement in the room, groups of relatives competed with one another, and they wanted enlargements, in color. In short, sales mushroomed. They could not get enough. The Irish, on the other hand, did not give a damn if the little bugger had pictures. Who needs them, they figured, he'll grow up and take them himself. African-Americans had a mixed problem, some wanted it; some would sign anything and forget about it the next minute. I tried it all, I did not last. Although I sold pretty well on the after-run, I forgot to charge sales tax. Since my sales volume was high, so was the money owed to the City. The Studio had to make it up. I got fired; they did not need someone to help them lose money. Who could blame them?

Well, I had a little gain, a bit more than I had before, a few bucks in my pocket and a car. What to do with the car? The subway was cheaper. During this fiscal period of mine I learned all about Chinese food, actually only about one food that I could afford, and of which Joyce introduced me to - roast pork fried rice. It was priced pretty much the same all over the city. It cost ninety-nine cents for a generous pile of a portion, covered by a Chinese style steel helmet with a Prussian spike handle on the top of it, to keep it hot. Tea was free; I needed another twenty cents for the tip. It was good and filling and I've loved it ever since.

Just a Pair of
Silver Candlesticks

Ever since I can remember, I've been looking at that pair of silver candlesticks. I vividly remember the spot where they stood in our home in Mannheim. I regarded them with awe and, as a toddler, was always fascinated by the detail of their design: the bunches of grapes on the base, the beautifully crafted grape leaves that were positioned neatly over them, and the curly stems. I liked to run my little fingers over the sharply formed bulges that added an almost realistic dimension to the grapes, bringing out their roundedness. The candlesticks stood on the highly polished chest of drawers and once a week and on holidays they were moved to the dining table where my mother lit the Shabbat or holiday candles. I looked at them a lot; their shape intrigued me and I never stopped wondering how they were made and who had made them.

Sometime later, we moved. We moved quite a distance. By train through Munich to Trieste, Italy, boarding a ship named Gerusalemme and sailing to Jaffa in Palestine. I had no idea where all this was and what we were doing there, except getting away from something my parents did not care for. I, though, liked the uniforms, the nightly torch parades, the colors and the flags all over. It was festive and noisy. I liked the train ride, too, the fact that we had sandwiches - not usually the fare I was used to - and it was fun, like one great picnic. The brown uniformed SA man who came through the train as we approached the border took the loaves of bread my father carried in a satchel, pulled them out and cut them up. I thought he wanted to make sandwiches too, but once over the border in Italy I heard that he had been looking for hidden money.

In Trieste I encountered more fun. We walked all the way from the railroad station to the port through winding streets. It got dark, and the streets, as we neared the port, lit up with lots of red lanterns, and lots of smiling ladies who called out to me "Bambino!" and to whom I smiled a lot in return. What nice people they were, but I was used to it, since practically everyone had been smiling at me throughout my short life.

My parents stopped a lot, carrying the suitcases and bundles and satchels. My father bent down to me and said that we had to walk and carry our own stuff, because we had no money left for taxis. When I suddenly asked what happened to the candlesticks, he replied with a slight smile, tapping one of the suitcases and said, "They are right in there. We saved them."

I can't explain it, but somehow this gave me a lot of comfort. I was on the verge of protesting the long walking trek, but somehow the news that the candlesticks were safe lifted my spirits, gave me energy and I marched on, not stopping until we arrived at the port.

The S.S Gerusalemme was sliding down the Adriatic, stopping in Bari, where there were half a dozen passenger ships at anchor taking on soldiers on the way to Ethiopia. I could not tear my eyes away from the spectacle of this whole army, tanks, trucks and cannons being loaded on. I was glued to the railing.

After five days on a choppy sea we anchored off-shore opposite the ancient city of Jaffa. It had no port except, I guess, for fishing boats, so anything bigger had to bob outside and be shuttled ashore in small boats. The suitcases, as ordered the night before, were all made ready and brought to the deck for the Arab longshoremen to unload.

My parents were busy with processing the paperwork and put me in charge of the luggage pile after repeatedly explaining to me in great detail, to sit on top of them and not to move. "Not a centimeter," my father warned.

"No matter what happens, you sit on top of this pile and stay. Just remember, the candlesticks are in there." My mother could not hold back reminding me once more of the same in her strictest command tone.

"But what if I have to make pipi?"

"Try to not think about it and hold it."

"What if I have to do something big?" I kept asking.

"Stop coming up with new ideas. Just do not think about it."

Well, I was hoping that nothing would happen, that no sudden urge would befall me. But what if it did? Well, after all, my sturdy Lederhosen would stand up to it.

I was ensconced atop the pile, looking out to the shore and at a landscape I had never seen before. Flat-roofed houses, piled like little building blocks with these funny looking church towers that I was later told were called minarets. The sun was bright and shining, the sky a speckless blue and the ship was gently bobbing at anchor. The Arab longshoremen, bearded, dressed in black loose pants with a tube-like thing sewn into their rear, were wearing odd-looking shirts and were barefoot or wearing old torn slippers and were running back and forth on the deck. Their shouts pierced the air in a language I had never heard before, coarse, hard, and unsmiling. I had to admit to myself that I was getting scared. In addition, I had to pee, and I guess the mixture of the emotions that ran over me at that moment expedited it. I did my best not to let it all shoot out, so I did it in as little spurts as was possible, holding on heroically to as much as my five year old physical efforts allowed. While I busied myself with this, a rough giant of a longshoreman, wearing those black pants with the tube attached in the back of his seat and a turban wrapped around his head, grabbed the handles of one suitcase and then the other, put the satchels under his arms and shouted at me when I tried to fight him. This happened so fast that my perspective changed in milliseconds; one moment I was here on top of a pile surveying the area from above, and the next, I was on the floor seeing nothing but feet, sandals, toes and shoes, from a bottom-up perspective and in wet pants.

I got up and started screaming. No one understood my German. "Die Leuchter, die Leuchter!" I yelled at the top of my lungs, watching the candlesticks suitcase disappear. The suitcases and the rest of our luggage sailed over the railing, straight overboard to a waiting longshoreman who stood in a boat down below, catching everything that had come flying off the ship.

There still was no sign of my parents. I ran around the deck in search of them and kept coming back to the same spot hoping to find my parents. On one hand I was keen to find them, on the other hand I was loathe to confront my mother. What was I going to tell her that the candlesticks along with the suitcases were gone, grabbed by one of these "wild Asiatic men," as she called everyone from Palestine?

Finally my mother came rushing by, telling me that she had to return instantly to the immigration authorities seated at the long table in the shadowy part of the deck.

"Where is the luggage?" she asked.

"Gone," I told her. "I do not know who took it, it was one of the wild men."

"Didn't you watch it like I told you?" she chided me, "…what happened? You had to go and make pipi?"

"Yeah, that too," I confessed, "…but I did not go anywhere. I stayed."

"What? You did it on the luggage?"

"I, I don't know," I stammered furiously.

"But where did these men take it?"

"I don't know, all I saw was them throwing it over the railing."

"With the candlesticks? You know they were in there."

"Ja."

A funny sensation crept over me at that moment, it was engulfing my whole body, my whole being actually. I started to hate those candlesticks with a passion I did not know I had. Up until now I had admired them, respected them. Suddenly all this turned to hate. "Boy," I mumbled to myself, "…if I get hold of these candlesticks I'll break them and then I'll throw them off the ship myself."

***

Three days later in Tel Aviv, we found a room to stay in and I started to reconnoiter the neighborhood, trying to find a kid my age. We now lived on Rashi Street, in the unpaved section. There was a sidewalk but no street. Actually the street itself was a pile of soft sand, good for camel traffic and donkeys, which traversed the area, but very hard for motor vehicles to maneuver. My mother had to go back to the port of Jaffa to retrieve the luggage from customs as well as the lift, it's what they called a wooden container for household goods, which we had brought along and were allowed to take out of Germany. In Jaffa she hired a horse drawn wagon to take the stuff to Tel Aviv. On that very morning, the Arab anti-Jewish riots broke out that lasted for three years, until the start of WWII. She got into the crossfire of the opening shots in the center of Jaffa. But she was so focused on getting her load to Tel Aviv that she was not fully aware of what was going on, as well as of the physical danger she was exposed to. That morning, mere feet away from where she was, four deaths and lootings had already been reported. Yet, she kept urging the carriage driver to get on with it. They made it and I remember standing on the corner of Peretz Chayut and Rashi Street seeing her coming, sitting up high on top next to the whip-wielding coachman. The first thing that entered my mind was, 'Gee, I want to sit way up there too.' The second was listening to the excited tales of people recounting what had happened that very morning in Jaffa. The dead, the injured, the burning properties, the refugees. As I said, my mother was oblivious to all that. She had one task, and that task was now sitting on the flatbed of the mule-drawn cart. Then to her utter chagrin, she discovered two bullet holes in one of the suitcases, and lo and behold, it was the one with the candlesticks.

"Die Leuchter, die Leuchter!" she yelled out. No one could stop her until she pried open the case, unloaded all the clothes that protected the candle sticks and retrieved them with a great sigh of relief. They were unharmed. Observing all this and being a bit embarrassed by the attention my mother had drawn, my hatred of these candlesticks only grew.

***

My father walked the streets looking for work or for something "to do," as he phrased it. "Needs a lot of looking around," he explained to me in his confidential manner. I loved it when he talked to me like that, we were sort of deep bonding. However, at that time there wasn't much "around" to look for things. The first half of the Thirties affected Tel Aviv like it did the rest of the world. The economic depression spread all over, and more so in Palestine where there was not yet an experience of prosperity to look back on. The local economy, anchored mainly by oranges, struggled to get on its feet. The wealthy and the ones who lived on farms and kibbutzim ate, while the rest of the population of barely six hundred thousand somehow survived.

My father and I would go to the open-air market at the edge of town, adjacent to the Yemenite quarter and on the border of Jaffa. The vegetable and food vendors closed their shops at sundown and cleaned out their sales tables. They wanted to get rid of what was left of the day's produce and so long as one took it away, they would give the entire remaining pile for the price of a kilo or two. We bought a hundred oranges for the price of ten, and lettuce, tomatoes, onions and even cottage cheese in packages. The problem was how to lug it home. Well, we would load up like donkeys, stopping to rest a lot on the way, then dragging it on the ground, sometimes taking off some of the load and leaving it in a corner or giving it to the beggars on the street and somehow succeeding in maneuvering it home.

My mother sprang into action and called on her rich brother. He had arrived a year ahead of us, but unlike us, he had risked it and smuggled his money out in the hollow of brass curtain rods which he sent to Poland and had then retrieved them from there. He invested his money building a major residential apartment house in the center of town with a slew of stores on the street level.

At the time of our arrival, he was in the midst of construction. After listening to my mother's tales of woe and how his brother-in-law was looking for work and had so far come up empty, he offered to employ my father as a construction worker in his building. However, only as a non-skilled worker, at the lowest possible wage, less than what the Yemenites were paid. They were much stronger he said and now replaced the former Arab workers who had left as soon as the riots broke out and refused to come back.

After a few more tries, my father realized the futility of looking for a job without "protekzia," the ubiquitous ingredient and trading currency for practically anything one needed, wanted, or had to have to stay alive, namely personal connections and a patron, such as a political party, school chums, family and recommendations by someone who knew a particular someone and many other someone's. So he hired on to build his brother-in-law's building on the corner of King George and Rashi Streets.

In Mannheim, dad had been a small businessman. I don't think he had ever exercised physically, and he had never engaged in heavy physical work. My father now had a very short commute, and it was a good thing for him since after a few months on the job, lugging bricks to the upper floors for the bricklayers, with a contraption on his back, made of a wooden board the length of his back and a short return on the bottom enabling two rows of bricks to be stacked on it, my father would not have had enough energy left for a long walk to work. It reminded me of the illustrations I saw in the Haggadah of Pharaoh's enslaved Jews before Moses got them out of there.

My uncle and aunt hardly paid any attention to me. They never offered me anything, except for lecturing me about the efficacy of the orange, that wonderful fruit, with which one can make juice and which one can eat at practically no cost. One could even eat the rinds, which were also edible and which could be dried in the sun. The rinds were full of vitamins, evidenced by the physical strength of the Yemenites who ate it all the time and the donkeys who gorged themselves on it.

Even at my tender age I understood that this man, my uncle, was not good. I told my mother, wondering aloud how it was possible that my grandfather, my hero and role model and buddy, could sire such a jerk. This upset her and the answer was a standard one that I would hear many times as the years went by – "Well, nevertheless, he is my brother."

Tel Aviv was small but construction was booming all over, yet there was tranquility in the air, a cross between a small town and a budding metropolis in the making.

My father's non-skilled salary was not enough for anything, certainly not for buying clothes for me if I was to go to school. Out came the silver candlesticks which were promptly marched off to the pawn shop. There was not much need for clothes, because in the summer it was close to furnace hot and it never rained. All that was needed were sets of light shirts, khaki shorts and sandals. I was still wearing Lederhosen and every kid I met asked about the fly and how it operated. It needs only be explained to people not familiar with that fashion contraption - the fly is locked by two parallel buttons on the top and once released opens up very much like a WWII landing craft into a generous square type rectangular opening. The German shirts were heavy, as were the knee-high socks and solid shoes. It all had to come off and it did.

The following week, my mother and I embarked on "school shopping" to locate a school for me. We never imagined what a job this would turn out to be. For five weeks, daily, in the hot, burning sun, we dragged ourselves all over town. The principals ran their hands over my head and remarked that I did not look too stupid, so they would consider taking me in, but not before I had acquired some fluency in Hebrew.

"How is he going to do this if he is not in school surrounded by his peers and other Hebrew speaking kids?"

"Lady, get a tutor. As I said, he does not look too stupid, so he'll catch on to the language in about two months."

"How much is a tutor?"

"I can't tell you that. You'll have to talk to a tutor, but probably a quarter to a half a pound per hour."

"My husband is only making four pound sterling a month. How can I afford this?"

"Lady, I am busy, and have to go back to my work. Good luck and don't worry, you've got a nice-looking kid there, and he doesn't look too stupid, so he'll catch on fast."

"Ima," I already called her by her Hebrew designation when we were outside, "…why does he keep telling you again and again that I do not look stupid?"

"Because he is. They all are." Thus, she dismissed the last one and all six principals before him in short order.

Totally frustrated after trekking for weeks all over town, and getting doors slammed in our faces, my mother got into a fighting mode. Someone told her that without banging on a table, nothing moves. The problem was which table to bang on? Where was this result-producing table? Then one morning, reading the German morning paper published by Blumenthal, she read a story that involved the city's education commissioner, one Lubianiker. Soon after, that same morning, we marched down Bialik Street all the way to its end, to the blue-gray curved Municipal building. The building was steps away from Mr. Bialik's house, the national poet and featured a colonnade on a second floor entrance section that was reachable via two parallel curving staircases, on the right and on the left and which converged on the top at the entrance lobby. My mother located Lubianiker's office and we marched in, like we were going to take over, or occupy the place. Lubianiker, the commissioner, had people in his office, glasses of tea spread out all over and two telephones. That impressed me. Two telephones? On our entire street there were no telephones. If one needed one, one had to go to the local pharmacy on the corner during open hours.

Lubianiker looked up as did every one of the half dozen or so people in the room.

"You are Mr. Lubianiker? You are in charge of education in this city? You are in charge of all the schools?"

"Do you speak Hebrew? I do not speak German and do not want to. What do you want lady? Thanks for giving me a list of what I am in charge of; I know what I am in charge of."

"See this little boy? I can't get him into a school. Do you take responsibility for the fact that he will grow up wild?"

"If you intend for him to use you as a role model, grow up wild he will. Get out of here before I call the police."

Now this was a big mistake that Mr. Lubianiker had made. As an entrenched member of the establishment and a brother of Pinchas Lavon, another high functionary, or as my father would say, "a Bonze" and who later became the controversial Minister of Defense in Ben Gurion's government and lent his name to an "affair," well this Lubianiker had it coming. My mother lifted a chair, a wisely-chosen one though, as it was one of the smaller, lightweight ones without the metal frame - and threw it at his head. It had to be admitted, that the man, despite his height, was agile and he successfully ducked the missile as a seasoned basketball player would. The hangers-on in his office instantly intervened, holding my mother back from killing him or causing more wreckage besides the already broken window behind Lubianiker that the chair had sailed through. She later suggested to the police outside, that had he not ducked, no window would have been broken. I was at first frightened and then I decided that if this melee continued, it would be my duty to join in. Accordingly, I was now surveying the office for things that could be thrown. Lubianiker whispered to the guard and waved my mother off. We left, but not after Lubianiker called out to my mother.

"Don't show your face again here, you crazy Yekke! Go back to Germany." My mother wheeled around in fury, but people stopped her from returning and finishing Lubianiker off. Chagrined and mad we withdrew, all upset and disgusted.

Then one day, our hikes in quest of a school led us to the very edge of town, to Bilu and Hashmonaim Street, to a leafy little patch, with a row of L shaped wooden barracks. The principal appeared, answering my mother's knock on his door. He was a bit elderly, and had lots of grey hair assembled in the back of his head, like a wreath framing his baldpate. I had seen pictures of orchestra conductors, painters and poets with hair like that. He wore glasses, a well-trimmed mustache and a yarmulke. He also wore a shirt with tie, as did all his teachers.

My mother started her routine, trying to get me accepted. Principal Mishori grabbed my shoulder turning it in a way that enabled him to look at my face without having to crouch down, looking for a long while and then cut my mother off in mid-sentence. Under usual circumstances this was treading in a forbidden area and not allowed, but in this case she stopped and listened hard to his broken German.

"First," he said, "…get him a hat. This is a Mizrahi school, it is a religious school. Second, he looks OK, could be even bright. How old is he?"

"Six and a half," my mother said.

Principal Mishori continued, "As far as the language is concerned, we'll drop him into first grade, let him float and I think that in three months he'll know the language."

"He already went through first grade in Mannheim, in Germany," she injected.

"Oh, we got a little scholar here! But this is Palestine, not Germany, so he'll have to start from the beginning. Do you know dear lady what Bereshit is?"

My mother tried in the swiftest possible manner to avoid the answer and to wiggle out of it. Principal Mishori was referring to the very first word of the five books of Moses. Bereshit means "In The Beginning." That's where I was.

"When can he start?" my mother asked.

"Tomorrow morning at eight o'clock. Bring him to the room marked with the big Aleph on the door. His teacher is Moreh Lifshitz. And don't forget a hat."

As we walked out, it took some time to absorb the relief of finally finding a school after a two-month search. We sat down on a park bench to collect ourselves and hugged. Then my mother decided that we would pass by Witman, the ice cream parlor on Allenby Street because we needed to celebrate. A wonderful idea I thought. Usually this happened only on the days when we went to the post office to collect the ten marks my grandfather could send us once a month as allowed by the Nazis then. But I was going to school now. "Like a normal person," my mother kept saying. No small feat.

"He never said anything about me not looking stupid," I noted.

"See, you can tell when you meet a civilized person," my mother now gloated. There was no higher compliment she could pay a person. To her mind, the "dwellers," and by that she meant the native born in Palestine, the Sab'res, were "Asiatics," - not too civilized, and so when she met one, who according to her criteria was indeed civilized, she could not shower him enough with compliments.

When I showed up the next morning at Moreh, meaning teacher in Hebrew, Lifshitz's class, he just led me to a desk and sat me down next to another kid, who turned out to be Arie Waksenbaum. The amazing thing was that Arie lived at Rashi 44 in a building owned by his father and I lived at Rashi 42, in a subleased room on the third floor of the apartment house, right next door, so we could go home together most days.

I got used to a lot in a very short time, except for one time, when I was convinced that the earth would open up and make us all disappear. One day, Arie put both his feet on the desk and leaned back with folded arms. Mr. Lifshitz came by, stopped and looked down at him. Arie did not move a muscle. After a few minutes, Mr. Lifshitz said to Arie:

"Waksenbaum, take your feet off the desk this instant."

"But I don't feel like it," Arie replied.

When I heard that, my mouth was left agape and my throat dried up. I came from Germany, where class discipline was surpassed only by army discipline. I was convinced that at such an incredible infraction of discipline, the earth would open up and swallow Arie and I would have to go home all by myself. However, nothing of the sort remotely happened. Mr. Lifshitz retreated, having given up doing battle with a bunch of six-year-olds, and Arie later took off his feet when he was good and ready, cracked his knuckles, stretched his arms and settled in his seat again.

Principal Mishori was right. It didn't take three months. After two months, I was well into speaking Hebrew without an accent and became part of a pretty respectable group of peers. Besides Arie there was Nathan Lakritz, whose family owned a bakery making bread. They lived and worked on a street parallel to ours. He was also the strongest kid in class and it was politically opportune to befriend him. He provided protection from bullies. Then there was Joseph Shivek, a very smart kid, who knew everything, and Israel Shafir, a font of knowledge and also of the smart set. He knew about everything before anyone even heard about it and sometimes walked with us. He lived way over the other side of King George Street opposite the Bezalel market, but in the same geographical direction as us. He wore a beret that was planted askew on his head in a devil-may-care fashion. It reminded me of my encounter with a beret. I first wore a beret in Germany when my mother drummed into me to keep one ear covered and the other exposed, thus controlling the angle of the beret. Then there was Eliezer Shachor, a chubby kid, very amiable and funny sometimes, who later got killed in the War of Independence. And who could forget the Avatichi twins, Menachem and Amichai, true and loyal friends with Menachem excelling in everything that was around to excel in, but who unfortunately became a casualty of the pre-War of Independence skirmishes.

My great desire, to still my passion, was for a bicycle. I never told my mother, but confided in my father.

"We'll see, be patient, before you know it, you are going to be riding the best bicycle in Tel Aviv, only I do not know when this miracle will happen," he advised.

At the Sarona terminus of Hashmonaim Street, which stretched from King George Street, traversing Rothschild Boulevard all the way to the Sarona fields beyond Kiryat-Sefer Street was where the Germans used to plow and tend the fields according to the seasons. Sarona was one of half a dozen agricultural settlements and villages founded by the German Protestant Templar Messianic sect in Palestine. Sarona was next to Tel Aviv, Waldorf was in the Jezreel Valley area and Wilhelma on the road to Jerusalem somewhere. There were also the German colonies in Haifa, Jaffa, Hebron as well as in the Galilee. The German inhabitants were Nazi sympathizers and members of the Nazi fraternities and their villages were hung with swastika flags, especially on Sundays. One day I stood at the fence and watched a young kid, maybe fourteen years old or so, driving a tractor and plowing his field. He waved and I waved back. Suddenly he stopped, jumped off his idling tractor and picked up a bicycle that lay abandoned in front of him. He piled it on the tractor and came close to the fence. He said something and I answered in German which of course gained his special attention.

"Do you want this bike, Hans?"

"My name is not Hans, but yes I want this bike."

"It is all rusted. So what's your name?"

"Alex."

"Good, but Alex, you're a little short for this bike."

"Don't worry, I'll grow. I'll eat lots of oranges like my uncle Julius says, and he is from Berlin, so he ought to know."

"Really? Is he Jewish?"

"Of course he is, aren't you? Why would he not be Jewish? But I better check with my mother. He is her brother you know and I think he is no good."

"That's it, must be Jewish," Wolfgang said. That was his name he told me. We shook hands and he told me that on Wednesday he would be out again and he would bring me a piece of the Heimat.

As soon as I got home, rolling the rusted bicycle next to me and not letting go of it, I asked my father what this Heimat thing was. I thought it was a piece of cake. After all he said he's going to bring me a piece of the Heimat, and I hoped it would be with raisins, I loved raisins in baked goods.

My father hated to be put into a situation at such an early stage and have to explain to his barely eight-year-old son the politics he was already being thrust into. He decided to do it at a later time. In the meantime, he said that I could keep talking to this Wolfgang, and get the cake from him if indeed it was a cake. But, he said, it is not called Heimat with or without raisins, Heimat was the land of your birth, and for all he knew, this fellow might speak Hebrew, too. It was nice of him to get me the bike, but if I ever heard him say "Heil Hitler" I was to immediately turn and leave.

The next task was to get hold of paint, as I wanted a red bike. I needed oil paint; actually this was the only type of paint for any outdoor jobs on the market then. I sanded and sanded and then I meticulously painted it with glossy paint and layered it on as thickly as possible, so it would last, I figured. I painted everything, the wheels, the handlebars, the frame, I wanted it all shiny red. I had the bike set up and turned upside down in the backyard, away from the lines of fluttering drying laundry. Every morning, I checked the paint and found it to still be wet. A week went by and the paint felt rather sticky now, not as wet as before. Another week went by and then a third, but I could not contain myself any longer. It was still a little sticky, but I decided to ignore it.

The time had come for the inaugural ride on my red bike. The next thing I planned for it was to get, somehow, a shiny bell. It rode pretty well, and I took off down the street at ever-increasing speed. I chose the concrete paved streets. I tried to ride it without hands, but it did not work because I couldn't get my hands off the handlebars, they were stuck solidly to it. I tried the brakes, but that was a mistake, as there weren't any despite my frantic backward pedaling. Then the bread truck crossed the intersection and I flew off the bike. It ripped my hands off the handlebars in a rather painful fashion. My first concern though was the paint damage to the bike. Smart kid. I landed on the concrete ground and chafed the side of my knee in a rather bad way. It bled and pieces of flesh hung off it. I collected my bike and limped to Mr. Levenson's pharmacy on the corner of Bilu and Luntz Streets. He knew my knee from past chafings. He iodized and disinfected it and bandaged it. The pain set in, growing by the hour.

The next morning it started to look worse. I looked at it and could not believe that it was my knee. My mother took me to the Hadassah hospital down on Balfour Street, pretty close to where we lived. The doctors concluded that if it did not improve, there might even be a danger of amputation. My parents of course went berserk. They took me home. The alternative was for me to stay in the hospital under medical care. But it was costly beyond my parents' means. I could see my father suffering and my mother ran to her brother but returned empty handed.

Again, it was a matter of money. There was a group of famous top flight surgeon- professors who could be engaged privately. My parents, after hearing the early verdicts of the hospital doctors, were beside themselves. Only the best and the very top would do, and save their son's leg. Money? It was back to the silver candlesticks again.

The candlesticks, our rotating asset, had just returned from the pawnshop, and were now rushed back into service. Back they went to that shop.

The doctors and professors did a good job. No amputation. In the end, I improved faster than was expected, and my accident left no impediments, and I could use the leg normally. After another few months I had completely forgotten about it unless I looked at the scar, which is still with me from what seems now millennia ago. I never found out what happened to the bike, and I never saw it again. I suspect my mother had something to do with that.

***

A few months later, we had a dire need for money again. My grandfather could no longer send any marks from Germany. The chronic shortness of funds plagued us again and the trusted silver candlesticks, just returned from the pawnshop, went back.

During the latter part of the Thirties, the candlesticks spent more time standing in the pawnbroker's store than in our room. By that time we lived on Kiryat Sefer Street, also in just one room but now with a terrace. It was tough, but I did not know it, I thought that's the way people lived in Palestine. In Germany, of course, I had had my own room, larger than the one in Tel Aviv, fully crammed with my toys. The present room we were in was also crammed - a double bed, a day bed that opened at night, a dining table, four chairs, and bookshelves. A box for the bed linen, a chest of drawers and when I got my first job as a fourteen year-old that came with a bike so that I could commute to work, the bike too was parked overnight next to my open daybed. But the terrace served as a room extension, where I could do my homework and entertain my friends. The terrace, however, was unusable during the winter and this became a real problem then.

The following year, when I was nine, I caught a cold, or so I thought. It turned out that I had contracted diphtheria. This was still the pre-antibiotic and pre-vaccine era, and kids dropped like flies from it, dying rapidly after being infected. My father was in a panic. It was the first time I saw him sit at the table crying. I had never ever seen him cry before or after about any calamity that hit us, but there he sat, all shriveled up in his desperate sorrow, glancing towards me, then turning and covering his face with his calloused hands and weeping. This really affected me as I could not stand to see him like that. It broke my heart and I cried silently into myself, and I was really at the very nadir of my usual optimism. What to do? I crawled out of bed, went over to him, put my nine-year-old arm around his neck and made him a promise that I won't die. He accepted it.

The idea came up to go to another expert doctor and to the hospital and make sure to get top care. The only thing in the way was money again, the source of my father's hopelessness and deep desperation. This time the silver candlesticks were still at the pawnshop. What to do?

My father decided to go to the shop, get an extension, tell them of the circumstances and make a deal. That's exactly what he did. This time he came back and said that the candlesticks would be gone for a year-and-a-half. We of course had no problem with it. With the help of the candlesticks I was brought to the top expert, a professor in his field who saw me in his private offices and prescribed the very latest modern remedies and then checked me into a hospital under his personal supervision. I quickly recovered.

Tough years. Oddly though, as the world political situation worsened, the economic situation in Palestine slowly improved. The Arab riots ended in 1939 and soon after World War II broke out and everything changed for the better economically, until it slid back down again after the war. But by then, I was getting out of school, became involved in the goings on, joined the labor force, earned money and hardly honored the candlesticks with a glance of recognition as they stood on the Shabbat dining table every week.

My feelings when looking at them were ambiguous - a mixture of gratitude and hate. These candlesticks permeated our lives to a degree we may not have been aware of at the time. They chaperoned me during my formative early years. They saved our lives, they saved my leg and they possibly saved me from chocking to death on the diphtheria I had. I could not help wondering what we would have done without them.

My parents wanted to give them to me when I married. I avoided it. I liked them; they were indeed delicately designed, beautifully crafted pieces. Every time I tried to compare them to others I saw of that style and type, I found them all wanting. They were of all silver, with no fillings, and perfectly done, yet light to hold up and completely hollow inside.

***

After my parents passed on and I lived in New York, I went back to Tel Aviv to settle their estate. It was then that I finally took the candlesticks and brought them back to my home. The more I look at them, the more I marvel at their gracefulness. I assume they must be close to one hundred years old, yet they look as if they had just come off the silversmith's workbench.

I relented on a recent Seder night, where they lent their magnificent presence and added to the festive table setting. Right after that, I placed them back on the shelves among the sculptures and other artifacts.

I cannot embrace them though. I'd like to still keep my distance, but hold on to them. I look at them and see the anxiety, worry and desperation piled up in them. And I look again and see how they so gracefully carried us all through it. Sounds pretty ridiculous to have such a relationship with a pair of silver candlesticks, but that's what it is.

Veracruz

When I once landed in Casablanca, I imagined seeing Humphrey Bogart and Ingrid Bergman. How could one not?

This time, landing in Veracruz, with the scenery pretty close to the movie, it did not take much to see Gary Cooper and Burt Lancaster in their Veracruz movie. Anyone who claims that we do not live the movies, especially when we get to places that do not look like the standard Middle America stetls, does not realize that we superimpose impressions we have learned about exotic locales from the movies. It makes us comfortable, gives us familiarity with a place and we are eager and ready to enter the exotica. Wow. What a place this Veracruz.

Coming up from the sweltering port and along the dusty roads, one is unexpectedly and pleasantly confronted with a lovely, leafy central plaza, surrounded by restaurants and cafés. Colorful cloth-draped tables with flowers in clay vases in their midst are protected from the sun by huge Cinzano stenciled umbrellas. Music, food and drink beckon one to plunk down one's overheated body in this oasis. All around it, the sidewalks of the arcaded buildings bustle with people, some rushing about, others just lolling around and men leaning against the columns savoring the fragrant Veracruz cigars. Wafts of barbecue with their little smoke trails and all those sizzling delicious aromas emanating from the sidewalk stands make one's mouth water.

At night, when the populace emerges from behind the lattice shutters, garlands of lights competing with the stars in the dark blue-black night amid the throbbing beat of the constant music. Life, which escaped from the sun all day, reveals itself. Families with babies, children cavorting, strolling lovers are all watched over by strategically ensconced old folks who knowingly observe the scene with critically trained chaperon eyes.

***

The reason I was there was to advise the governor, my third governor so far. Veracruz is a big and wealthy state. John Monahan, a well-known travel industry executive, had got me there. He was one of the most handsome men to walk the earth and who, after hitting the Normandy beaches on June 6, 1944 with a few hundred thousand others, had decided that when he came back he would keep hitting beaches. And he did. All the resort venues up and down the Caribbean, Florida, and Mexico and everywhere on the tourist trek benefited from his trade expertise. John wanted me to meet with the governor there and explore how I could assist in the planning and the establishment of a tourism industry in Veracruz.

Unlike the State of Guerrero on the Pacific coast - with its star Acapulco, its natural beauty, and well-developed by former president Aleman into a world tourist destination and where tourism became the main industry for lack of other resources - Veracruz had quite a lot of other business. Oil, cattle, coffee, vanilla, cocoa and important port business. Yet the Governor wanted to add international tourism to his economic portfolio. I had always loved Mexico, but I had never been to the Caribbean side of it until now.

The state's capital and the government seat were up in the hills, in Xalapa. Raul Villarosa, my appointed expediter, was a charm-oozing, fast talking, well-traveled fellow, a man about many towns in both hemispheres. He claimed that he was well-versed in the latest happenings in Paris, London, Frankfurt, Zurich and Rio de Janeiro, as they were happening and before they happened. He had never missed a carnival in Copacabana and had credible bikini fashion expertise. He was an aide and confidant to the governor and would chaperon me during my stay.

The few hours it took to reach Xalapa by car from Veracruz on the shore, was an incredible demonstration of the climate variances. Where Veracruz was sizzling hot, hence Gary Cooper's tropical garb in the film, and mostly bearable when evening and night settles, Xalapa was a cool, verdant hill town and a very comfortable place. With an almost European tinge to it, it is home to an array of classical cultural institutions. A large university, concert halls, an archeological museum that rivals the major one in Mexico City, cafés and student hang-outs, all were part of the city's charm and character. And of course it is the State's governmental seat and that of the governor, who presided in the Palacio de Gobernador, located in the center of town, next to the central plaza.

I was assigned two rooms in the hotel, one to serve as my office and an English speaking secretary. Food was available at any time from the kitchen, and bar or room service in the event that I might have guests in need of libations.

"Well, when will we meet with the Governor?' I asked my liaison officer the following morning.

"Any day now, any day."

"What do you mean any day?" I cried out.

"You'll see, take it easy, have a cigar or eat a mango."

His Excellency Governor Dante Delgado Rannauro was a relatively young man. The only time I had seen him so far was on the local news.

Tradition went, I was told that a governor of Veracruz is on the path for Minister of the Interior, a very powerful position in Mexico and from there, the path extends in a straight line to the presidency. I listened and liked what I heard. This governor then was laden with heavy potential. Time would tell. I'd had this happen to me before, in Georgia. Was this becoming a habit? If so, my fees would have to be substantially increased if I was to start peddling presidential futures.

With time on my hands and no meeting yet in sight, I started walking about this lovely town. I was exploring the University, checking out the student body and the beautiful hilly campus, when a car came screeching to a halt, practically on my shoe. It was Raul.

"Dr. Kaufman," he yelled out, "...after dinner tonight, we meet the governor."

Raul had taken it into his head to call me Doctor. I have no idea why, and the more I told him to desist, the more he did it. All the others, from the drivers to the crowd of people toiling in the offices we visited, the hotel staff, now called me Doctor, regardless of how many times I waved them off. They took it for a sign of modesty on my part.

"What time are we going to see him?"

"Oh, in his office, in the Palacio. Maybe around twelve."

"That's midnight?" I gasped.

"Yes, we don't want to waste any time, do we?"

"No, perish the thought, absolutely not."

Well, I did not care, so long as I'd be able to get some movement going here. If it couldn't be made to move during the day, then let's see what could be achieved at night.

At midnight, Raul picked me up and showed me into the governor's office on an upper floor of this huge Palacio. Lights were on and I saw some people at their desks. Others clustered around, talking, as we passed. Raul called out to them and they were smiling and waving at me, so I smiled and waved back as well. We went through these enormous twelve-foot-high doors into the governor's office, a large, spacious place, a little smaller than a football field, but I don't think by much and behind a desk, at the end of this immense room, sat the governor. He looked very pleasant and friendly in jeans, an open collar shirt and a leather bomber jacket with a cigar stuck in his mouth. He got up, came around, invited us to sit down in the chairs in front of his desk, then swung up onto the desk and sat on the edge of it.

"The governor wants to know what you think of Veracruz," Raul told me.

As the governor nodded in agreement, I tried to address him direct-ly. He smiled some more. It became clear that English was not his language; he understood it, but did not speak it.

"OK," I said, "…I'll talk and you react in Spanish."

"OK," he said.

Slowly I got the gist of what the governor had in mind. In brief, alt-hough there was no sort of official memo, he wanted Veracruz to have an international tourism industry, just like Guerrero. He wanted his state to be known all over the world. He wanted international conferences, tourism investment seminars, hotels and investors and wanted to promote the state as a super tourism destination.

"They made a film here, right outside, up in the hills," Raul translat-ed.

"A film? What kind? You mean the one with Gary Cooper? I know, I saw it a long time ago."

"What Gary Cooper? He's dead. Not that one, they just made it. It's called 'Romancing the Stone' with Michael Douglas and Lana Turner."

The governor energetically nodded his head.

"Lana Turner?" I said. "She must be very old, is she still alive?"

They consulted, they called in a fellow, and a lively discussion en-sued among them.

"It's not Lana, it's another Turner."

"Not important, it shows Veracruz scenery," Raul proudly pro-claimed. It occurred to me that he had something to do with bringing the film to Veracruz.

"But it plays in Colombia, I hear," I had to inject.

"No Colombia, we are Veracruz," the governor repeated to make sure, thumbing himself on his chest.

"It's OK, it does not matter. At any rate, tell the governor that I have not yet seen anything of Veracruz except a bit of the city and the ride up here."

The governor offered me his helicopter for a few days, to go and run through the state and to see the sites. Do I agree?

"Yes, of course. And once I have had a chance to view the sites, I shall prepare and submit a report to you."

"Thank you, very good, great help," the governor told me in English.

***

With the business part over, we all sat down in front of the desk, stretched our legs, the governor slid his shoes off and we relaxed. Raul knew Sly - that is, Sylvester Stallone - and treated us to a credible imitation of Stallone's manner of speaking. Cigars and tumblers of cognac appeared. The custom of dipping the cigar tip in the cognac was not bad, I had to admit. The governor's English had now miraculously improved. Lots of laughs, and the cognac was excellent as were the cigars. What is there not to like about this place and its governor?

By three-thirty in the morning, having run out of stories, we broke up the convocation. I had a feeling that I had entered the zombie zone. I was dying to sleep. Any kind of work schedule was blown to the wind.

"I'll call you when I wake up," I told Raul. Good thing he did not put a time on it.

***

On a flat surface pad, a few hundred feet from the governor's office, I climbed into the waiting helicopter.

"Tell him where you want to go," Raul yelled, cupping his mouth.

Well, I had earlier scanned the map, read up on it, consulted with the local tourism official and made a list. El Tajin would be number one. It is a tremendous pyramid complex, second, I suppose, only to Chichen Itza in the Yucatan. El Tajin is located in the northwestern part of Veracruz. It is in the rain forest area, another tourist attraction.

El Tajin is indeed a marvelous site, stretching over two thousand six hundred and forty acres. It consists of a grouping of pyramids centered around the Pyramid of Niches soaring to significant heights that dominate the area. Intricately sculpted panels and sections of the pyramids reveal sophisticated artistic skills and craftsmanship. Structural sections were made of poured concrete, such as overhangs and roofing. It was all part of a city that flourished in 600-1200 C.E.

Then there were the famous Voladores de Papantla, a Veracruz sensation, exhibiting daring flying feats as they circle and unwind themselves, descending a one hundred and fifty-foot pole. They are tied to ropes and clad in their traditional colorful costumes of the Totomac people. It is a world-renowned tourist performance.

***

El Tajin, in ancient times, was strategically positioned on an important trade route to the sea. Religious practices guided its culture. It featured seventeen ball courts, with sculptured panels depicting the sequences of the game and the human sacrifices to the gods.

The nearest town was Papantla a bit further to the northwest. El Tajin was an extremely rich and impressive site. Although not on the popular tourist routes, it had been visited by millions of tourists for the past hundred years. It is, of course, unquestionably, the number one tourist destination in Veracruz.

Hovering along the beach I sighted a fisherman's shack, walls and roof covered with palm fronds. The fisherman was barbecuing his catch. Since it was close to lunchtime, we descended and proceeded to have an excellent lunch of assorted seafood, just brought out of the sea a few feet away.

After five more days and after visiting the spectacular hillsides, the coffee plantations, of savoring the food, exploring the river sites and spending time in the city of Veracruz, I was ready to discuss preliminaries with the governor.

We called for a breakfast meeting one morning on the patio of my hotel. It was an absolutely lovely spot, situated on an elevation overlooking the scenery for miles. Colorful sun umbrellas guarded the tables adjacent to the pool, competing with the color bursts of the flowers arrayed all around. Palm trees that lend a tropical atmosphere completed the picture. In the background loomed a snow-capped mountain. The combination was intriguing and would make an enticing picture for any future tourism promotion.

I took the governor by the arm and guided him to the viewing spot from where I would want the picture taken.

"Yes?" he questioned, looking at the scene.

"Look at this magnificent view. Imagine it as one of the Veracruz's promotional pictures. There aren't many places where you have a tropical paradise topped by snow-capped mountains. Look at the beauty of it all. Tourists will be drawn to it."

"Can't be done," he said in a very definite tone and led the way back to the table and our breakfast.

"Why not?" I insisted, completely puzzled.

"Because it is not our mountain."

I needed a few moments to digest this.

"Who cares whose mountain it is? We are not inviting anyone to climb it. Can we borrow it for the picture?"

He now looked at Raul and the two other aides he had brought along. I was looking at them, too. They were trying to gauge the mien on his face. As trained "Yes-men" they needed a hint on how to respond.

***

"We'll let you know. We'll think about it."

The big reception party, launching the tourism idea for Veracruz that Raul had planned and arranged, was scheduled for Friday night. It was now the topic of discussion. It was going to take place on the plaza and in the garden of the Palacio, really terrific venues for an affair like that. Colored lighting was being strung, fireworks were being prepared and, of course, Mariachi bands would play. Food and drink would be served buffet style on long tables. It all took me by surprise.

"What do you think, what do you think?" an excited Raul kept asking me.

"I think it is a great idea. I am sure it will be a blast."

"What do you think?" the governor chimed in, turning to me.

"Great idea," I said, "…although a bit premature. We don't have any specifics to offer that can be followed up, except to tell the world that we want to do it."

"Right!" the governor called out, slamming his hand on the table in front of him. "Right!" he echoed himself.

"Governor, how many people will be there?"

The governor looked at Raul, who without missing a beat said, "A thousand or so."

"Sounds good. Who are these people?" I asked.

"Hotel executives, bankers, tour operators, the usual travel business people and, of course, the travel press," Raul filled in.

"It's the right mix," I said, "…but don't forget the Port-a-Johns."

It was actually Raul's idea from the start. We were on the same page on this subject. The governor was puzzled until Raul explained the logistical details to him.

***

Three weeks later, I was up in Xalapa again. I brought with me a preliminary plan and proposal. The night I arrived I was invited to a gala concert. It was a festive event, men in black ties and women in flowing evening dresses. Flowers abounded. The place was aglitter.

"This is for the start of our tourism project," Raul told me. "Stay here, stand next to the governor greeting the guests."

So I was doing as I was told in my khakis, blazer and tieless. I counted two ministers from Mexico City, one general and his girlfriend, the richest man in Mexico and the cream of the local society. Festive and beautiful.

The orchestra was made up of Polish musicians. Seems there was an influx of them in Xalapa. Raul told me that they all jumped ship one day in Veracruz, escaping the Communists. The concert was magnificent. The governor was a happy man.

"Raul," I said, "…you'll have to buy yourself a hat to stick all the deserved feathers into."

"Tomorrow we meet with the governor," he told me.

"Great, that's why I am here."

In the morrow, we indeed met with the governor. This time it was earlier, at eleven p.m. I asked for an easel to make, what might be called today, a PowerPoint presentation.

"First of all," I told him, "…the need for a tourism industry in Veracruz is not critical because of all your other resources and established industries. However, if you insist, it will require a long-term commitment, proper funding to establish it and then more to sustain it in the long run competing for the international tourist dollar. You will have to compete aggressively too, with Guerrero and Acapulco as well as the other established tourism sites here in your own country. It is a tough ladder to climb, but it can be done. It will take money, lots of it and time." They looked at each other, not having expected this.

"So, if you choose to pursue this plan," I went on, "…then do so with no holds barred. You will have to recruit international and local investors, have the federal government participate with the financing, tax abatements and incentives. Before all that, the first thing you will have to do is build the infrastructure – roads, lookouts, tourist friendly environment, beaches, restaurants, hotels, sightseeing services, car rentals, boat rides, rental facilities for water sports and fun, as well as annual tourist events and festivals. And you will have to initiate a top training program for personnel that would attend to all these activities and services."

The governor was looking at his cigar. He looked like he just took a cold shower. Raul was trying to save the day, or the night as it were.

I tried to cheer him up.

"Governor, it is remarkable what you want to do. If you do it, you will go down in history. But if you do not do it right, it won't have a good ending. Your local business community must stand firmly behind you, raise money for it, get investors, this is the key. We shall help you," I said, looking at Raul who was hiding behind the cigar smoke.

"Let's work on it," Raul finally said. "Give us some time; we'll see you next month."

"Good idea," I replied.

And we proceeded to have our now traditional cognac and cigar dipping session. Raul regaled us with his exploits and adventures in Europe. The governor loved it; he had never been to Europe and surely will go one day.

***

I was back in Xalapa again. Almost felt at home there. I had brought with me a story board for photo shoots. Raul had hired a photographer from Guatemala. I chose sites and activities that could become magnets for tourists. Producing a selection of photographs and videos, since introducing Veracruz was a necessary first step. El Tajin and the Voladores, horseback riding on the beach, the food, water-skiing, surfing, the rain forest, mountain climbing among coffee plantations, the romantic ambiance of Xalapa and the exotic make up of Veracruz city were all to be part of the content.

*****

For six more days, we rode around in the helicopter, with the story board and the Guatemalan photographer. The scenes were designed to speak for themselves. I believe they did.

While waiting for Raul, I settled for the five o'clock in the hotel's café. A lovely indoor place, serving Viennese coffee, so it says on the menu, and strudel. It was a very European atmosphere. A five-member ensemble of Polish musicians performed medleys. Some I may have met before at the concert. There were three men and two very blond ladies, with violins, an accordion, a bass and a clarinet, presenting a repertoire from Bach to Kurt Weill and back. The men were dressed in suits, the ladies wore something resembling 'dirndl's' and all were wearing sock-less sandals. They were very nice people, lending a whiff of worldliness and certainly a welcome addition to this town. Still, it was sort of on the edge of being out of place, it certainly was an unusual make up consider-ing the place and the offerings. A juxtaposition of Vienna in Xalapa and executed by Polish musicians in sandals, with their toes moving to the rhythm while playing German and Austrian music.

The governor was in an expansive mood. He slapped every back in sight. He kept coming back to the party.

"I wish we could just do a few more receptions and get this tourism done that way," the governor proclaimed. "That was good. That was something. What a party. But the idea of the portable toilets, that sure saved the day," then pointing his cigar at me, "…you really earned your money with that. Hmmm. Just imagine?"

And I thought it was about establishing a tourism industry. So I shall be remembered for the portable toilets. At least in his mind. What if he becomes president one day?

One never knows where the praise comes from or what ignites it. Any token of appreciation is, of course welcomed. I guess the important part is that someone pays attention. And my governor sure did.

I've Got the Money What Shall I Do with It?

It was late August, two in the afternoon and the sun, in a speckless blue sky, was literally boiling the runways of this former British RAF base. We were in a flat depression between the Mediterranean and the rising hills to the east of the Biblical Samaria. It must have been one hundred-twenty degrees. There was no way to measure what it was in the shade - there wasn't any.

The airfield and its former RAF base had been evacuated by the British shortly before May 15, 1948 but, like many British bases sprinkled throughout the land, it was not formally delivered to either the newly minted Israelis or to the Arabs. The bases were left dangling like prize mice with two cats constantly ogling them and calculating to pounce and grab them. Well, this base was no different and we pounced and took possession of it.

We were two squads, left behind to hold the airport and guard it. The thought occurred to me that this was either an irresponsible act or an extreme vote of confidence. It was probably neither as it might have been for lack of a better choice. We were a rather motley crew. The squads were formed from remnants, or as we called it, leftovers, from units decimated in battle and who were under strength. We were mostly Hagana veterans, the pre-state mainstream security organization, which became the army. I came from the Latrun battle, a debacle where we practically lost everybody. We were all locals, born or brought up here and we were all in our late teens. Joining us were a slew of Palmachnicks as a result of Ben Gurion's disbandment of the Palmach, the legendary commando unit founded and trained by British Brigadier Orde Wingate during WWII to act as a behind-the-lines guerilla unit in case Rommel overran Palestine. They were all farmers and Kibbutznicks and political-ly on the far left. Joining them were their political rivals on the right, the former Irgun and Stern gang members, also disbanded by Ben Gurion and dispersed all over into army units. This brought about an embarrass-ing situation for me. The former Irgun commander of the Tel Aviv region, a celebrity in folk lore, was assigned to my squad. I kept apolo-gizing to him, but Naphtali, a very solidly built fellow of about thirty-five years old, was very gracious about it.

"Will you at least advise me?" I kept asking him.

"Of course," he said, "…we will advise each other."

To add some color to this team, we were further joined by a group of freshly arrived fellows, just repatriated from the British detention camps in Cyprus where they had been held after being intercepted some months before by the British Navy, when they were trying to break the immigration blockade on rickety ships from Europe. Lastly, we got a small contingent of former British 8th Army and Jewish Brigade veter-ans, mostly in their late thirties and forties, "old guys," who constantly wore a bemused look on their faces as they watched our attempts to masquerade as an army unit.

They were good; they knew what they were doing. I decided early on to watch them and learn. And then there was our radio man, a heavyset, jolly fellow who came via Machal - another Hebrew acronym for overseas volunteers. He had volunteered from Ireland. Never saw him without a smile. When he was not fumbling with his dials and buttons, he was equally busy foraging for food. What a face, topped by a bush of red hair, smiling and chewing.

Cliques, dominated by language were immediately formed. I was in charge of one squad and I had fifteen guys I felt responsible for. It dawned on me that the orders I was issuing were not being understood. Yiddish, however, seemed to transcend the Polish, the Russian and the Hungarian languages. I was a quick study. Yiddish was easy as I already knew German, but it was hard on Ezra, the Yemenite Mem-Kaf of the other squad. Mem-Kaf was the acronym for Mefaked-Kita, or squad commander. We used the rank designations from our Hagana days where exterior-worn symbols of rank did not exist, and we had not yet received any official army rank insignias. I also picked up some Russian, especially the curses. We had a couple of Red Army veterans who used to put on a competition of who could curse the longest without repeating himself. Well, Kushner won - thirteen minutes by the watch. However, with the Persian, the Turkish and the Greek languages we both had trouble. We just left it to body language. A very difficult task in the dark and quite impossible by radio.

On one side of the airfield camp was a pretty densely populated Israeli area, actually the midsection of the country. We were a short distance from Hadera, which sat half-way between Tel Aviv and Haifa on the Haifa Road. East of it, next to the Tel Aviv-Jerusalem-Haifa railroad tracks was Kibbutz Gan-Shmuel, a very friendly lot who used to invite us to their parties on Friday nights. From there, one went along the pretty straight leafy road to the corner of Camp 80, which was the designation of a former British armor base. A sharp left in a northerly direction led into Pardess-Chana and a newly established tent city housing whole families of new arrivals from the Cyprus detention camps as well as from European DP camps. Passing this branch and off to the next right turn in the road was Gan-Hashomron and further down the road was the large and well established Kibbutz Ein- Shemer on the left. A few hundred feet further on the right, was the entrance to the air base. A short distance beyond was Kibbutz Ma'anit, sitting on a hillock, almost in line with the hills framing the eastern perimeter of the airfield. This was where we set up our observation and defensive outposts. It denoted the border line between Israel and Jordan, which held the territory at the time.

We were facing the Triangle, so named after the three major cities in this region – Jenin, Nablus and Tul-Karem, or as the Triangle became later known - the West Bank. On the other side of the border to the east, the Samarian hills rose abruptly. Spread along the width of the crest and facing us was the large village of Baqa-al-Garbiyeh and the adjacent smaller village of Gat. Iraqi troops, part of the invading forces sent by the six Arab countries to expedite the Jews into the nearby Mediterranean, were garrisoned in the villages and occupied the heights, stretching all the way south to Tul- Karem and Kalkilya, about eight kilometers east of the seaside city of Netanya, the narrowest spot on the spine of the new state.

We watched them and they watched us. They had artillery; we made do with shelter trenches. We saw them daily, lined up during their morning parade, each figure an ideal sniper target. It was eerie to expose troops on the horizon like that. We never tried very hard to pick them off, because we didn't have snipers nor the right tools for it and then there was another reason, we did not want to provoke their shelling.

Their cannons were positioned out of sight and they just loved to engage in fireworks at the slightest whim.

On the main road, down from the corner of Gan-Hashomron, the prosperous, private enterprise village founded by German Jews who ran a very efficient farming business and expressed disdain of our unkempt and unruly appearance and who always came to our camp accompanied by the Military Police whom they summoned, accusing us of stealing their chickens, which they could never find and which arose their ire even more. Some of the more outspoken members of our squad lifted their shirts and baring their midriffs, invited the "Yekkes" to x-ray their stomachs. This wasn't so far off the mark, because that's where the chickens were.

To say that the personnel of our squads was varied is definitely an understatement There were worlds of difference in ages, education, personal backgrounds, cultures, mind-sets and life experience. We had Nazi camp survivors with the most horrid experiences. Wachtel for example, a smart, very blond good looking kid, about my age and size, was piggy-backing on his father when they ran away from a German raid in Poland. His father was shot from under him. Wachtel, in shock, then not yet eleven years old, lay on top of his dead father till nightfall when he awoke and walked away. Yevgeny claimed that he was a tankist in the Red Army and was an expert in finding bureaucratic loopholes that we did not even realize existed. Belzer had a mania for bread, hidden in his belongings and in his pockets; you'd always find bits of bread there. Then there was Marcel Kaufman, a waiter from Paris. I liked him and not only because we shared a last name. And there was Slivovitz, who claimed that this was his name and sat a lot by himself and took to laughing attacks, without cause or reason. And Strenger. He must have been the oldest judging by his looks. He was bald, the only baldy in our squad. He exuded a calm wisdom that stood out among the blank faces the rest of us had. He told me that he lost his hair in Tobruk, where he had been under siege for many months, and then was taken prisoner by Rommel until freed a short time thereafter. He claimed that he had had his helmet on for all this time, never took it off, and that it had caused his hair loss. Then there was Hooshang, the Persian barber; he sported a goatee, long sideburns and an arty pompadour-like hairdo, all in pitch black. All he wanted was out. This was not for him. He was used to the better things in life. "Why did I come here?" he kept asking himself, loud enough so everyone could hear him. He cut our hair and, while doing so, never talked about anything else but "I want out." Then he spread the word that he had Syphilis. Now everyone wanted to know if it was contagious. Or, better yet, could you catch it when he touched your hair? And of course there was Bakalash, I think he had no first name, no one ever called him anything but Bakalash and that seemed alright with him.

From a military perspective, we were a very loose bunch. It did not perturb us because, as was said, coming from the Hagana where units were small and informal, one did not know much about the rest of the organization. This was purposely so in case we were arrested by the British. The less we knew, the less we could reveal. But this was an army; we were out in the open, bearing arms. Well, it did not bother us very much.

The two squads, Ezra's and mine, constituted this military unit and our responsibility was to hold and guard the Ein-Shemer airfield. We did not belong to a platoon, a company, let alone a battalion. The Alexandroni brigade was in charge of the overall area, and it had a battalion stationed not far from us, I think it was the 37th, where we were told to go in case of a medical emergency. The bulk of the commanders were from Hadera and I knew some by name and reputation from my earlier visits there. While other brigades were busily active in the Galilee, Jerusalem, the Negev and down to Eilat, Alexandroni's front was pretty dormant. There weren't enough resources available then, and the central front was put on the backburner.

One day a bunch of Chimnicks rolled into camp, stopped in front of the former British camp commander's office and started unloading stuff, looking like they were moving in. It was an administrative unit. It consisted of a captain, and his adjutant, a lieutenant. This was the first time I saw what the rank insignias looked like; they had them neatly placed on their epaulettes, brand new. Two more Chimnicks ran back and forth, with no clear idea why. A word of explanation regarding

CHIM which begot the Chimnicks of this story. CHIM was a Hebrew acronym to Cheil Matsav, the ch was pronounced with a throaty sound, unlike the English ch; it meant Garrison Units. These units consisted of people, partly volunteers, who were above the conscription age, but wanted to participate and were needed for behind-the-lines, non-combat services. They were all over, and they had skills we needed. There was a saying: "Say hello to your dad, he's over there talking to your grandfather."

So these two Chimnicks, done with their running back and forth and who could have been our fathers, wanted to know what we were eating. They must have been in their fifties, ancient. One was a cabdriver from Ramat-Gan, the other a matchmaker, pretty well known through his weekly ads in the papers, but not as famous as Lieber, who was also a Chimnick, and as well a leader of a military band that he also farmed out to weddings he arranged.

Yehoshua Licht from nearby Hadera was the captain in charge. In his civilian life Yehoshua was a scrap metal dealer and one could determine right away where his love interests were. Yehoshua never met a rusted pile of twisted metal he didn't like. If one walked with him along the camp's perimeter, it was uncanny how he would spot a piece of scrap hidden between the undergrowth and instantly, like a recorded message, he'd begin saying "How do I get this to my yard?"

We also had three British Army Bedford trucks in the camp, still with the RAF markings on them. Yerucham, our expert in all matters automotive, was a Tel Aviv municipal garbage truck driver. He inspected the vehicles and announced that we had only two trucks, the third was a pile of junk and he'd use it for parts. Well since this was one man's opinion there always existed the possibility that somehow this truck could be brought back to life. A dire prognosis may have excited Yehoshua and before we knew it, he'd have the truck cut up for scrap. Sometime after we made a tank out of one of the trucks and used a lot of cannibalized parts from the third truck, like Yerucham said. But this was later.

Yehoshua's group brought along a cook, that's at least what he said he was, a few Shin Gimels-Battalion policemen, two drivers and a recent immigrant who had just arrived from a DP camp in Germany and kept yelling that he was no soldier.

"So what are you?" we yelled back.

"A tailor with a diploma. I was once in Paris, I'll have you know."

I called Marcel to test his claim.

"On which street did you work?" Marcel asked.

When the tailor told him, Marcel, the former Parisian, said he never heard of such a street. Well, we put him to work. We never received uniforms, so we wore our own clothes, we needed repairs, and at the end the guy was a godsend.

Back to the sizzling August afternoon on the Ein-Shemer airfield. As per our routine, Ezra's squad was manning the three outposts, numbers 7, 9 and 11, called Mishlatim in Hebrew, on top of the hills, while our squad was at rest. The camp had about two dozen low-slung brick buildings, topped with a Quonset-type curved corrugated metal roof. It was a standard British design, found in all British bases all over the world. It was efficient, and I guess that wherever British troops were, it made them feel right at home. However, when hit by the sun, the roofs became furnace hot. Were these roofs not sharply curved, they could have been used as cooking platforms. We kept all the windows and doors wide open, hoping to catch any whiff of breeze that might come by. My squad was lying on their makeshift bunks and straw sacks, exhausted, sweating and snoring away the afternoon. The sun kept beating down, there was no wind, not a leaf turned on the tree outside.

Suddenly the stillness was broken by a distant drone. I immediately identified it as that of an airplane. We were getting bombarded I con-cluded. Maybe by the Egyptians, or the Jordanians. I don't think the Iraqis sent airplanes over, but then what's the difference whose bomb hits you. With that in mind, I ran along the barrack, banging on the bunks, waking everyone up, yelling for them to grab their rifles.

"Have Salman grab and load the MG34," I shouted, "…and get out and look out for the planes." The drone became louder, ever closer as it slowly approached us.

"What the hell is it?" I kept asking myself.

By the time we were outside of the barrack and starting the trucks, it grew into an ear splitting noise, and then it was right on top of us throwing a shadow. I was looking up and saw it coming down on us, rather very low, this big, huge white airplane. I had never seen such a big plane in my life. In truth I loved airplanes. I had always been an aviation enthusiast; I had wanted to get to the air force. When I asked for it, I was typically assigned to the infantry. I had been a junior member of the Tel Aviv Glider Club, running along the beach after a pick-up truck and trying to launch a glider that was tethered to it. In total fascination I kept following this big white bird and I could clearly read the three big blue letters that spelled KLM with a little crown on top and a legend above it in another language.

We were now all up from our crouching positions and silently followed the plane, and lo and behold it was coming down on one of the runways, went to the end of it, turned around and came back, then stopped.

"This plane is from Europe," Strenger, the one who lost his hair in Tobruk, said knowingly.

"It sure is not from Rosh-Pina," Bakalash piped in, referring to a tiny village airport up north.

"Hey, get the trucks and let's get down there. Now!" I yelled.

We had the two Bedford's and an ambulance that happened to be in camp drive down to the runway. One truck and the ambulance faced the door of the plane, the other truck positioned itself on the other side of the plane. 'Well, if nothing else, we have it surrounded,' my strategic mind thought.

Standing in front of the truck, I noticed that the window where the pilot should be was sort of ajar, but there was no one there. Then the door flew open and there stood this blond guy, in a white shirt and dark pants, fanning himself with a magazine in one hand and holding a bottle in the other. I waved to him, he waved back.

"Want a beer?" he called out.

"Yes, yes," I answered. This could be the best thing that had ever happened to us ever since we came to this place. Before I knew it, a green bottle of ice cold Heineken was sailing through the air, right at me. My audience, to emphasize their empathy for this manna that just came down from heaven, was standing there with their tongues stretched out in an unmistakable message.

The pilot disappeared, and my guys, suspicious and careful, trained their guns on the door. Instantly he came back, dragging a box with him, and shouting in English, "Come and catch it." And he kept raining down beer bottles.

"You could not have come at a better time," I yelled up to him in German. He woke up to it and we started a conversation. He beckoned me to come closer. We drove the truck under the plane, aligned it with the door, and I climbed on the roof of the cab while the Dutchman sat down on the floor of the plane his feet dangling outside of it. Now we were only a few feet apart.

"I brought you the money," he started, "…my name is Joppe, what's yours?"

"Alex," I said.

"Alex, I just came from Amsterdam; I want to get out of here as fast as I can. This is a war zone. By the way, where am I? Is this Lydda?"

"No Joppe, this is Ein-Shemer."

"Are you Arabs or Israel? Man if I lose that money I'll never hear the end of it."

"No, we are Israel, I mean this is Israel, you are in the right country but it looks like at the wrong airport."

He took another swig from the green Heineken bottle, shook his head, nodded and said, "It wouldn't be the first time, ha, ha, ha," topping it off with a few more swigs.

"Joppe, what's this money you mention? What do you mean by money?"

"Didn't anybody tell you? I brought the new money, all the money that's going to be used for this new state of yours. This money is instead of the old British money you have. I've got all the money for the whole country, right here," and with that, he patted one of the boxes like one would pat a dog or a cat. "Nobody told you?"

"No, I still don't understand, but if you say so, OK. Well, how much is there?"

"I don't know. Who knows? Millions. Trillions. I did not count it and have no intention to." And he bellowed again. "Ha, ha, ha." This guy was the nicest, friendliest and most loaded person I ever met.

"Alex, you got to get me out of here, before dark. Please unload, and get your forklifts."

"Joppe, what's a forklift?"

He threw me a panicked look. "You don't have forklifts?"

I was really not familiar with the term, I knew dictionary English, never came across a forklift and had no idea what a forklift was, or meant, but figured it must have to do with the mess hall since he mentioned forks.

"Don't worry, Joppe, I'll check with the cook."

That killed him. He must have given up on me.

"No, no, get your people to work, get going, in a few hours it'll be dark, I've got to get out of here. And tell me, can I make a turn over the hills there?"

"No, you better not, there are Iraqis there, they may shoot you down, just go the way your plane is pointing, straight out to sea."

"You got any controls here?"

"What controls? What do you need controls for? Just fly straight."

He flipped open one more bottle, looked straight into my eyes, saluted and called out, "Yes sir. But now get the damn money out of my plane."

I got down, told my guys what I had learned and what we had to do. For the next two hours, we unloaded the money. The plane was almost empty. As a reward everyone who wanted to, could climb into the plane and look around. Like me, many had never been on a plane, let alone a giant plane like this one. It was a DC-4. It was huge. There was beer in this plane to the rafters. Nothing better could have hit us on that broiling day. Nobody paid much attention to all that money.

"Money, money," sang the pilot's sidekick, another blond giant who was munching sandwiches all the time and which he offered all around.

I decided to pry open one of the boxes, Yerucham had a tire iron and voila, neatly stacked, under oil skin paper, with little bands around the piles, was money. I pulled out a note, it said State of Israel/Bank Leumi and it had a big number five in the corner.

"See, look at it," I said to Yerucham who was still standing there with his iron clenched in his hand. "This is the money for the state, replacing the English money. Remember you saw it here first."

Surprisingly, no one tried to grab any money or even thought of doing so. They enjoyed the ice cold beer more.

Amazingly, no one in the country seemed to be alerted about the plane, even though the pilot came down at the wrong airfield. No one was looking for the plane. How many airfields were there? You'd think someone would have checked them all out? Nothing. Now I was trying to think real hard, the hardest I ever thought in my life. Here I was, a Mem-Kaf, two months over nineteen, making twelve liras or so a month, sitting on all the country's money, holding it, responsible for it, under my sole control.

'What are you going to do?' I kept asking myself, then bursting out, "I don't know, I don't know."

Slowly, I formulated a plan. First I must get to Yehoshua and tell him to get some guys to relieve Ezra's squad, so they can come down and rest. I would be busy with the money and didn't know yet how this would shape up.

Yehoshua had just come back from Hadera. He didn't hear the plane but promised to take care of Ezra. He had got a troop of Chimnicks from Hadera that he was going to call in and send up to the outposts to sit there.

The next step was to talk to the Magad, another Hebrew shortened word for the rank of Mefaked Gdud, meaning Batallion Commander. I knew one by the name of Shemi, I had met him months before in a café in Hadera. I knew that he was with Alexandroni but had no idea which battalion he commanded. He might have known or maybe he'd have been told by now. I tried to raise him on the radio. The Irish volunteer radio man finally got him. I was hoping that he knew all about the money and would be relieved by the news of where it was and then would promptly dispatch his men to pick it up.

"Hey Shemi?" I started. "I got the money what shall I do with it?"

"Who is this?"

"This is Alex, the Mem-Kaf from the Ein-Shemer airfield."

"Who are you?"

"I just told you. Are you Shemi? The Magad?"

"I'll ask the questions. Who is your commander?"

"Don't have one. We are here two squads."

"What are you doing there?"

"What am I doing here?"

"I'll ask the questions, I told you."

"We are here to watch this place so the Iraqis don't come down from Baqa and take it. You didn't tell me what to do with the money."

"Talk to the Shalish, I don't know who you are."

"This is Shlomo, what the hell do you want? Is this a joke or something, what's your number?"

"90527, Mem-Kaf."

"What unit?"

"Don't have a unit, used to have one though."

"Did you get wounded in the head?"

"No, but what do you want me to do with the money?"

"Spend it, asshole."

The radio guy ran his finger across his neck, indicating that the line was dead.

I was sitting on the pile of neat orderly boxes, with all the money of the State of Israel under me. What do I do now? Whom can I ask? Maybe dump the whole thing in the sea, it's about fifteen, maybe twenty-five kilometers from here, no one will know, they'll just order another batch and this time Joppe may find Lydda.

As I was mulling this over again and again till my head hurt, I looked out over the camp and airfield. It had been inactive ever since the British left in May. During World War II it was an important base for bombing sorties targeting the Ploesti oilfields in Romania. The operations barrack was still undisturbed with the names of the flight crews and all the related pertinent information was still on the chalkboards. Today, our plane had reactivated it. It had to happen on my shift? The wind-sock was torn, and permanently pointed towards the south-west which happened to be the direction to Tel Aviv. "That's where we should go," my crew had bugged me in the past. There was no chance for leave, somebody had to stay here; otherwise in no time, the Iraqis up the crest would come sliding down, and take the place back.

I kept looking at the windsock and it suddenly came to me. 'I've got the money,' I reasoned with myself, '…where do people put money? In a bank of course. Do you know a bank? Yes, I do, one in Tel Aviv.' I glanced at the windsock again, saluted it. Yes, that's where we were going to go. Actually, I did not know any banks. No, never did business with a bank, but, I had a classmate who worked at a bank; I used to visit him there often. So that's where we will go.

My whole squad was now gung-ho. They had not been to the city in many weeks, tonight we were going, we could not delay.

"I must get rid of the money," I explained to a chorus of "Yeah, yeah, yeah, we better." They all agreed.

We got a small convoy together made up of the two Bedfords and the ambulance that still held the money ever since we unloaded it from the plane, two pickup trucks and two three ton trucks Yehoshua got us and with Yerucham on a motorcycle he had filched from somewhere.

Off we went. After clearing Hadera and turning left we barreled down the Haifa-Tel Aviv highway, going south. We stopped at the Bet Lid crossroads.

"Where is this bank?"

"It is at the very end of Rothschild Boulevard, after you cross Herzl Street. The name of the bank is Ellern, it is a private, very good bank." How did I know? I didn't, but it was the only bank I'd ever been inside of.

At about forty minutes past midnight we finally arrived at the Bank Ellern. Our parked motorcade took up the entire street. Good thing it was nighttime, no one else was parked there and the whole area was deserted. I walked up to the door, trying to get in. It was locked. My squad on the trucks wanted to know what was going on.

"The bank is locked, it's closed."

"Of course it's closed," the older guys called out, "…it's after midnight, what do you expect?" Admittedly, I had not thought of that.

"Why don't we lock the trucks and go home or down to Hayarkon Street to the bars."

"Good idea, when do you want us to be back?"

"Well, they open at eight in the morning; it says so on the door."

"Great, see you." And before I could blink an eye, my squad disappeared into thin air.

I circled my money caravan one more time, and then walked home, the keys to the trucks buried deep in my pocket. My mother was delirious despite the fact that I got her out of bed. She started with food and finally by three in the morning I fell asleep.

Eight o'clock the next morning, my very groggy squad was arrayed outside and lingering on the stairs leading to the bank's portal. I did not realize that we had our rifles and Stens on us. Accompanied by Strenger and Bakalash, I walked into the bank. As we entered, the place fell still. I could not find any face that I remembered from times past. I asked for the manager and then noticed the frightened faces of the staff.

"What's going on here?" I asked Strenger.

"WE are going on here. They think it's a hold up."

"Get out of here, that's nonsense."

The manager came out, his face as white as a sheet. It suddenly occurred to me what we must have looked like to him. I think they thought we were really holding up the bank. I went close up to the manager, put my hand on his shoulder, an act none of his long time clerks would have ever dared do and told him that we were not holding up his bank, just the very opposite, we want to put money in his bank, more money than he had ever seen in his life. He looked at me, glanced over to my two companions, looked us up and down, took a step back, nodded his head and said, "Of course."

He invited us into his office and we sat down. I told Bakalash and Strenger to better leave the weapons outside the room. Strenger, the mature fellow that he was and a German, explained in the best German that I could never have mustered, to the German speaking manager what this was all about.

"I have to make phone calls," the manager said. Then he started with the third degree type of interrogation.

"Who are you?"

"We are in charge of Ein Shemer airfield. Ask Magad Shemi." I volunteered.

"Who gave you the money?"

"Joppe, the KLM pilot."

"How much is there?"

"No idea."

"Maybe it's fake?"

"Maybe."

"Anybody lift any of it?"

"Why would we? It might be fake."

He now looked at me at length, squinted his eyes, furrowed his brow and in a suspicious tone said, "Don't I know you from somewhere?"

"You might, I used to come visit my friend Becker, here."

The manager stopped for a minute, rested his chin in his hand, and said, "Aha. Do you have receipts?"

"You haven't given me one yet."

The manager was suddenly on the verge of a panic attack. "How can I give you a receipt, I don't know the size of the deposit," he screeched. I got the urge to torture him a bit.

"Just write BIG, in big letters."

He of course had never heard of anything like this, he was never told that all these monies would come to his bank.

"Whose decision was it to bring it here?" Bakalash and Strenger proudly pointed at me. "Why did you choose Ellern?"

"Because it is the only bank I was ever inside of."

"Do you know sir," he addressed me, "…what it takes to deposit this money?"

By that time I was hungry, I had not had breakfast yet, coffee would have helped a lot and some food. I mused. 'How did I get into this? What had befallen me?' I was trying to do an honest job and for that I got driven out of my mind. 'What does it take to get rid of money?' I started to get mad.

"What did you say? I do not give a shit what it takes to deposit this money. Do you know what it took to bring it here? Do you know we drove all night? Do you know that we are hungry and sleepless? So don't give me your excuses; they won't fly. This is the money for the State. Now tell your clerks to get off their fat asses and get this money off my trucks and in here…and fast."

The manager stiffened, his face turned the color of beets, and he looked at me, then at Strenger and said to Strenger, "This young man is not a gentleman."

"We know. You are absolutely right. He's crazy, better do what he wants." Strenger eagerly agreed.

The bank's floor was about five feet off the sidewalk with semi-round steps leading up to it. There was no loading gate. We pulled the trucks up to the glass door, opened both doors wide and unloaded the boxes and had them stacked to the ceiling. The procession lasted for some time, the bank employees, assisted by the squad, were walking back and forth, carrying the white pine boxes. Finally the trucks were empty; we were ready to ride back. As we pulled out, the police arrived.

"Where is the problem?" they shouted, wanting to know.

"In there, in the bank, fellows!" we directed them.

We drove by the Beazlel Shuk, the market place and the best Falafel venue in Tel Aviv. We stocked up on it, gorged on it, then hopped back on the trucks to pass by Sarona, or the Kirya as it was called, to gas up at the military pump station there. We had no vouchers, but we had some Heineken left in the trucks.

I still couldn't get over the whole affair. The Ministry of Finance should have paid for the whole thing, and where were they?

On the ride home back to camp the guys started talking. "You know, you may end up in jail," they assured me.

"Look what a hard time you had getting rid of the money, wait till they find out how you grabbed it by the truckload."

"Making money is a lifelong battle, but who'd have thought that to get rid of money is even harder? This is nuts," one guy lamented.

"You think this is over? It has not yet begun," one of the older 8th - Army veterans pronounced, "…and you know why? Because the higher-ups screwed up, and they are probably out there looking for the money and they haven't got a clue where it is. So you, our little Mem-Kaf, will be the convenient scapegoat, watch till it hits the papers."

On these cheery notes we rolled into the camp. As we went up the little incline and pulled up in front of Yehoshua's office, we noticed a group of armored cars lined up there with people milling around them. One of them peeled off the group. He too, wore one of the brand new rank insignias; he had a falafel, as it was universally called, on his epaulette, a yellow fig leaf denoting the rank of major. As he approached the first truck he started screaming.

"Who is in charge of this gypsy caravan?"

"I am," I replied as I stepped out, "…what's going on?"

"What's going on is what I want to know," he yelled.

"Who are you?"

"I am the commander from Camp 80, from the 7th Brigade. We need the trucks, what did you do with them, where were you?"

"These trucks are ours, what do you want with them? We were in Tel Aviv on an important mission."

"On an important mission?" he screamed, his voice breaking. "What, to see your girlfriends, to visit mama?"

"Yeah, that too, but we were on an important mission as I told you."

"What's your unit?"

Here we go again I thought. "This is our unit including one more squad resting in the barrack."

"Who is in charge?" he said through his clenched teeth.

"Me and Ezra. You know, sometimes me, sometimes Ezra."

"What is your rank and where is it? I do not see it."

"I don't know exactly what it would be in stripes, but from the Hagana yet, I am a Mem-Kaf. And actually, we didn't get the ranks and insignias yet. What is your name by the way?"

"You want to know my name? I am your Mefaked, that's how you address me."

"Fine, but you are not my Mefaked. I do not belong to you."

He thought for a moment, digesting this whole silly conversation. "Thank God," he finally muttered under his breath. He then came closer, whispering into my ear, "Would you please let me in on it, Mr. Mata Hari?"

This guy was the type who echoed conversations. Everything I said he just repeated with a question mark, then he got the gender of the spy wrong.

"We took the money to the bank," I whispered back into his face.

He looked at me, choking on his saliva, opening and closing his mouth, finally throwing up his hands, turning, walking away, then stopping, turning to me again, "I am not finished with you." And he walked off.

I was about to answer him, but Strenger grabbed my shoulders, turned me around and pushed me in the other direction.

"What's this guy want?" I blurted out.

"Forget it, he likes you."

Minutes later, a whole squad of his came trotting over, jumped into the front truck and drove it off to the clearing and stopped next to a welded frame contraption made of water pipes that they now lifted and placed over the truck, with only the very bottom of its wheels showing. Suddenly, I noticed an outline of a tank and before I could think any further, another crew unloaded bales of jute fabric, sack-colored and clipped and then stretched it on to the pipe frame. Before my eyes, they turned our truck into a tank; I mean you could think it was a tank from a distance.

Strenger came running, all flush in the face, "Hey, that's what we did in the Libyan desert, it's camouflage. Wait, where is the stove pipe that gets stuck in the front and then all the ropes with the chains on it and the empty cans to drag behind to work up dust. Oh, we did it all the time."

Indeed that's what the guy with the falafel from Camp 80 wanted the trucks for. They told him that we had them, so he brought the frame and the jute and his 8th Army camouflage mavens over. Everything was ready except the trucks. Then when the trucks finally showed up with this weird crew, they told him that they had to go to Tel Aviv to the bank to make a deposit. So was it any wonder why he blew his top?

The Alexandroni Brigade commanders figured that tanks should be paraded on the fringe of the camp and airfield, to put the Iraqis up on the crest on notice that we too had tanks, after a company of Iraqi tanks suddenly appeared on the horizon. It was to lend the impression that the airfield was protected by more than just two motley squads, and was rather heavily armed. So from the next morning on, our 'tank' started to make the rounds, raising a huge dust cloud. We had it disappear behind the two story hangar building and appear in rapid succession. Maybe they'll buy the fact that we have more than one tank. Stranger things had happened. Strenger stopped it at once because the stove-pipe cannon was not adequately fastened and bounced up and down as the truck moved along. In one of the barracks we found a fishing rod the British left behind. We extended it with a bamboo stick and fashioned a pennant for it and stuck it to the 'turret' of the tank, according to Strenger.

The 'tank' was successful; as a matter of fact it was too successful for its own good. It drew heavy fire. It was being shot at all the time, which created another problem, of who was going to drive it? It got to the point where no one wanted to stand anywhere near it. Every time the argument ensued as to whose turn it was to drive it, Bakalash always volunteered. 'I'll do it for a while, and then when you done arguing, I'll come by and you take over." And that's how it was.

After demobilization and returning to the more or less normalcy of life, I just could not help looking at the new Israeli banknotes in people's hands, without a knowing smile. These used to be all mine for a while, if they knew the trouble I had to get them into their hands. Eerie.

The Great Diversion

Early on a non-descript, mundane Queens morning, the men came. Suddenly the street, populated by an assortment of businesses, came to a standstill. Only a minute ago people had been starting the day, bustling with vehicles coming out and going into driveways and loading docks. Now the street was paralyzed.

Crews of city workers, clad in orange-yellow vests and clutching coffee cups were all over the place. They were posting large, green directional signs for new approaches to the bridge leading to Manhattan. Done with rearranging the traffic pattern and establishing a new one, they were gone as suddenly as they appeared, without giving it a second look. And understandably so. Who in his right mind would hang around and linger to watch the monumental mess they had just created?

Obviously, trying to improve traffic in a congested, crowded area is like an amateur trying to assemble a Rubik's cube. You transfer bottlenecks from one place into another place where it does not fit either. A dog eventually catches its tail sometimes if only for a short moment, and this too, might work after midnight for a few hours. It really defies solution, no matter the volume or amount of traffic you factor into your graphs. Traffic has a peculiar nature, it grows exponentially, there is always more and it never diminishes.

By ten o'clock in the morning, around the time for a second coffee, the street was blocked. A solid wall of trucks and trailers was planted along it. All of them were lined up along the street to reach the bridge. There were cement mixers on their way to Manhattan, with their goods drying up in their drums, cars and vans of all shapes and sizes, all insistently sounding their horns in a pitch that could awaken the dead. The smell of diesel accompanied by exhaust vapors permeated everything. It was well-designed mayhem.

Vendors, peddling every imaginable relief for the frustrated drivers, popped up seemingly out of nowhere. Coffee, donuts, sodas, sandwiches, cakes and apples made the rounds. One guy ran along with a Sushi plate doling out one roll at a time. A pair of vendors carried pizza boxes. The ubiquitous Chinese food containers also appeared, along with vendors hawking newspapers and lottery tickets. They all chased each other up and down, doing a land office business and practically falling over each other while attending to the open driver's windows and the dangling stretched out hands clutching dollar bills and expecting the goods.

Overwhelmed by the noise that sifted through the walls of the buildings, people came rushing out. The minute they hit the sidewalk and caught the air, coughing and sneezing started, preventing anybody from talking in long sentences.

"What's going on?" What are they doing here?"

In reply, someone pointed to the freshly installed brand new green signs that invited the traffic to come down the street prior to entering the ramps to the bridge.

"Why, that's crazy!"

Coughing and sneezing, the consensus settled into vigorous body language, nodding of heads and arm flailing common to gestures of surrender.

Queens Plaza, where all this occurred, is a major subway and trans-portation hub in New York City's Borough of Queens. It is closest to Manhattan and, at its western end, it runs straight into the Queensboro, Midtown, or the 59th Street Bridge, or you can call it now the Ed Koch Bridge. It deserves the many names it goes under. They are all true. Every veteran crosser has his own designation for it; few know where the Ed Koch Bridge is. Call it what you want, it is a major artery and it seems that everyone wants to get on it. Rivers of cars, buses, trucks flow over it. You can also take a short, scenic walk across it - some aficiona-dos call it a stroll - and it will land you smack on 59th Street and Second Avenue in the heart of Manhattan. Travelers from Manhattan in the direction of Queens may go there for business or proceed to the Long Island Expressway, the rather funny name for what New Yorkers call a parking lot, the Parkways, the bridges, nearby LaGuardia airport or further out to JFK, to Brooklyn, the sports stadiums and to Long Island. Queens Plaza is indeed an important crossroads and key hub.

Going West or East, the side streets off Queens Plaza running north to south feed and absorb the incoming and outgoing traffic that con-verges on Queens Plaza. It supports the run-up to the bridge and the traffic that comes off it.

This is where our saga began. We were in a commercial building on one of the crucial side streets, about fifty feet as the crow flies from the Plaza. It was a coveted location. Our building, as well as the other buildings adjacent to it, were replete with businesses of all kinds. Woodworking shops, food distributors, garment makers, distributors of toners for copy machines and printers, truckers, jewelry makers, music purveyors, distributors of food and fruit products and of endeavors too numerous to mention. We had loading docks and driveways for vehicles to enter and leave at all the hours of the day and night. It was a busy street and not a small bellwether for the economy of the City.

We and the rest of the street's inhabitants stood there, helplessly observing how our breathing was getting chocked together with our businesses. In history books such situations are described as a siege. It became even more discouraging when one of the foreman of the orange-yellow vested battalions, told us that this was a diversion only. It was not to be a long lasting project, just maybe six months at the most. Now this was a load off our chests, the siege would only, repeat that, only last six months at best. Very comforting. So why don't we all, everyone on the street, go on an extended vacation or a six-month cruise around the world. My suggestion was not understood by all. English was not everyone's language in Queens. A simultaneous inter-preter from the UN building right across the river would have helped. Nonetheless, by acclaim and vote, and aided by vigorous slaps on my back and energetic head nods, I was anointed leader and spokesman of the besieged, a career move I always coveted, now I had it.

Back in the building with business on hold, time was available to call for help. My tendency and instincts have always been to go to the top. Reagan's trickle-down theory, starting at the very top, is very effective in such cases. It saves time and has a high rate of success. The top in this case was the president of the borough. I immediately put a call through to her office and after a bit of back and forth, I was able to speak to her assistant, a very willing and cooperative lady. I gave her a brief descrip-tion of the calamity that had befallen us, the street and its businesses and asked for an early meeting with her boss. Within a short time we nailed down a meeting for that coming Thursday, at eleven o'clock sharp, in the Borough's President Office in the Queens Borough Hall at the eastern end of Queens Boulevard.

Plotting out the meeting in my head in preparation of meeting with a public figure and a politician, I knew that I needed a critical mass to make an impact. Volumes of people impress politicians, lots of people means lots of potential voters. As I walked into the various business establishments along the street in an attempt to recruit my 'troops,' I felt that the enthusiasm to protest and lay out the grievances had abated. There was a lot of shifting from foot to foot and many tried to wiggle out of it. The recently immigrated business owners were suddenly loath to march on the government; repercussions they remembered from the countries they left were still fresh in their minds, memories from their past in China, Romania, Russia, Iran, India, Afghanistan, Turkey, Bulgaria, and Croatia were vivid. At the end of the day, many were afraid to demonstrate their civic rights and try to correct a government measure.

"Why aggravate the government?" they kept asking.

"They will put us on a list and we know from experience what can happen to people on the list. And altogether, our English is not adequate," piped the Italian carpenter, who lived a few blocks up and had only been in the United States for the past twenty-eight years.

No sense fighting a lost situation, only thing left was a compromise. Easier said than done. I started with a speech about freedom and civil liberties but stopped after looking at the faces around me that spelled out... 'Sure, it's easy for you to say, we've heard speeches like this before and we are not going to take any chances.'

I now put on a serious, what I hoped would sound like an official tone, and told them that I had registered their names with the Borough President's office and that they were all expected to show up. Not honoring the time of the meeting would result in a waste of time for the president and might make her very angry.

Resistance started to melt as they argued among themselves in their various languages. Tones rose, shouting ensued until I stepped in and informed them that we needed 'numbers.' I counted ten business owners; we needed fifty to seventy-five people. My tone became more insistent. "So get your employees, your friends, your wives your suppliers and make up this number," I urged.

They stood there subdued, chain smoking, to calm their nerves I suppose, and took it in. Would they deliver on it? 'On Thursday we shall know,' I reasoned. Lastly, I informed them to assemble at ten-fifteen sharp on the Subway train station around the corner from our street.

In my office hung this large, poster-sized airline calendar printed on nice glossy paper. I tore off a month and on the backside drew a map of the traffic pattern in black and red markers and a solution to it that would completely unblock our street. According to this plan, 28th Street would return to its original purpose, namely serving the plethora of businesses located on it.

I invited my son, who had just graduated high school and was hanging around the office for a few days during his vacation, to come along and partake in the opportunity to witness government and the people in action. He got into it enthusiastically, was all over place like a fish in water. This worked well as we now had an additional body in our protest delegation.

On the designated day and time our fifty-five plus contingent marched into Borough Hall. Once in the lobby and directed upstairs to the Borough President's conference room, they became rather quiet, some holding their caps and hats and trying to slide unseen into the room. As we entered, a row of chairs at the long conference table was already occupied. There were not enough chairs around the table, so the chair-less were happy to line up against the wall, with the hope of blending into it. The room was nicely filled and one could say that we made a show of force in terms of human attendance. The very efficient assistant, who had helped me thus far, came in and a little flabbergasted look crossed her face when she saw the mob of people. She intended to ask if anyone was game for coffee or a soda. Suddenly, my troops came back to life, and started to ask for tea, green tea preferred, Dr. Peppers and all sort of sodas unknown to me and some of which I heard of for the first time. The Italian carpenter, who before had claimed that his English was not presentable, flawlessly articulated his expectations of refreshments, such as cookies or finger sandwiches. A hapless mien swept over the assistant. Coming to her rescue, I reminded everyone of the purpose of this important and crucial meeting. That we had come to talk, not to eat and drink. However, refreshments could be bought in the lobby on the way out. Business first I declared firmly, food later. Had I not done this, within minutes, this convocation would have turned into a chewing, munching, slurping free-for-all. The assistant, the burden lifted off her shoulders, threw me a look of gratitude and left.

Within minutes, at eleven o'clock sharp, she reappeared again, announcing the entry of Mrs. Claire Shulman, the Borough President of Queens.

Mrs. Shulman impressed one immediately as a no-nonsense top executive of high caliber. Unusual for a politician. She cut through all the double talk, hot air and small talk. She literally grabbed the bull by the horns, would not let go, until she received a sensible, satisfactory answer.

A trait that is directly opposite to the mentality of the large and extensive bureaucracy she was heading.

We were introduced to the other people in the room, who occupied the row of seats at the conference table opposite us. Mrs. Shulman had done her homework and had her people from the various departments present. There were managers and experts from the Department of Transportation, traffic engineers and planners, police captains of the area's precincts, as well as people from the sign department. They were the ones who had hung up the signs all over the place the other day, the source of the problem and the raison d'être we were there.

"OK, let's go," she said after delivering a preamble, addressed to her department representatives, asking why they were congesting a street, hampering the pursuit of business, and doing so without any advance notices to the business community, a critically important yet now adversely affected tax base.

The traffic engineers opened their satchels and pulled out graph after graph, computer printouts of traffic patterns, statistical back-ups replete with acronym type, notes, codes and explanations. In no time, the length and width of the conference table, and a rather large one it was, was covered with these color lined papers. She picked up one or two, studied them, then looked up and asked, "What am I supposed to deduce from looking at this bowl of spaghetti?"

I thought that our moment had come at this particular moment, so I pulled out the calendar sheet and presented our solution as I had drawn it on the back. It showed 28th Street, north of Queens Plaza, with a diversion of traffic through streets south of the plaza, a less crowded area which could offer more than one street.

Mrs. Shulman grabbed the paper, looked at it, asked me a few questions and wanted to know whether if we made a slight change, would it be acceptable? From our point of view, anything that would not encumber our street, was of course acceptable.

"Why do I understand this plan and not your spaghetti plan?" she demanded of the traffic chief, who looked at me and regarded our troop with growing antagonism. Good thing he was not packing a gun.

"OK, let's go with it," she said. She was about to get up, when I mentioned the signs.

"They have to come down, right now," she pointed her gaze at the head of the sign department. "Can you make a set of new signs, so this whole mess gets straightened out according to this plan?"

"Yes," came the subdued low-voice answer. She threw me a look and nodded her head.

"Please Mrs. Shulman, please ask him when?" I pleaded.

"When?" she thundered.

"Wednesday," came back the little voice. Well I thought, today was Thursday, next Wednesday would not be bad. But past experience arose my suspicion.

"Please Mrs. Shulman, please ask him which Wednesday?"

"Next Wednesday, right?" she asked.

"N-e-x-t Wednesday?" came back a reply of total astonishment in an incredulous voice, repeating himself, "…next Wednesday? Impossible!"

"Which Wednesday did you have in mind?" she continued.

"Well, two or three weeks from today maybe."

"Glad I asked, let me tell you, get all your sign painters together and have these signs up by next Wednesday. Anything beyond that is an abuse of taxpayers, a hindrance to business, and people will sustain losses. We cannot tolerate this in Queens; we are here to help businesses to thrive. Understand? Next Wednesday then."

She stood up. It was a powerful statement, almost a political speech. The politician came out in her. We hit a nerve. All we wanted was to keep pursuing our businesses without hindrance by government or planners who sit high up in ivory towers and have no clue what results their drawn color lines might beget.

I thanked her on behalf of my now hungry, refreshment deprived assemblage. I shooed them out and explained to them outside, that we had sort of won. Once the new signs were up on the other side of the plaza, relief would be complete. Some walked stoically. Most however straightened up and now walked erect, quietly, proud of their encounter with government and that they were listened to.

What was of course remarkable was the 'can listen and can do' demonstration of this wonderful Borough President. The following Wednesday, the street reverted to its normal hustle and bustle, new signs went up, traffic went over to the other side and stayed there during the ensuing six months it took to finish the construction.

My son enjoyed himself. He had sat at the conference table, observed it all, and exchanged a few words with the Borough President, who asked him about his schooling. Her daughter became an astronaut who went on space missions. He delivered observations of the various people in attendance, the managers, the lower rungs as well as the mannerisms of members of our contingent.

At the end of the day it firmly instilled the value of democracy, teaching our immigrant business people that there is nothing to be afraid of when seeking your rights. That you can get the attention and the ear of the very top officials. Not always, of course, and not every time might you meet with a Claire Shulman, but this should not prevent you from trying. They are people like you that you elected and that you have the power to vote them out of office, too. An exercise of democracy in action. They could not stop talking among themselves. They had met the highest official in the borough where they lived and worked. The street was still under siege at least till the following Wednesday, but their faces were happy. Man, that was something, wasn't it?

The Coronel went to War
Back Mañana at Four

As I looked out the airplane window, I had to look twice and rub my eyes - there, practically level with me, was a peasant woman, in colorful garb, hanging laundry on a line strung between two trees. The first thought that raced through my head was that we were crashing. I looked around, but everything looked normal, then the announcement came over the speaker telling us among the usual instructive litany, that we were about to land at the Quito airport. I then realized how spectacular this descent was, flying between inhabited mountain ranges, and unlike flying by the Alps or the Rockies. I saw villages, animals grazing, people walking, children running about and waving to the plane, one of many probably they saw passing by. It was a most spectacular sight and must be a quite difficult descent when coming in for a landing.

Quito, at nine thousand three hundred-fifty feet in elevation, is the highest capital city anywhere. With a population of one and a half million out of about fifteen million for the entire country, it is a busy city perched on hills with a rather pleasant climate, although it sits smack on the equator. The climate does not vary between the seasons and is steady year round.

***

I went there by invitation of Colonel Hidalgo, who was in charge of housing. There was great interest in our Italian designed construction method and my concept of catering to local design and customs when building houses, rather than trying to adapt the design of imported prefabricated housing elements. The idea was to buy the machinery that would produce the construction material, thus addressing two needs – housing and economic development. The machinery would be owned and operated by local entrepreneurs and labor. Industrial training to operate the computerized machinery as well as on-site construction training were part of this concept. This would of course provide long term business that could further develop into exports as well as skilled employment as an alternative to importing. This was the purpose of my trip to Ecuador.

***

At the airport border control Colonel Hidalgo awaited me and with a big abrazzo welcomed me to Ecuador. He was a man of medium height with a commanding manner and attired in a crisp white shirt and dark blue slacks, surrounded by four aides who immediately picked up my luggage and we all drove into town and my hotel. I liked the guy. He had an open face and a personality to match with an easy laugh. I didn't always know the reason for the laughter but I figured laughing is good.

The Quito Hilton was perched on an elevation in this hilly city, recessed from the main road. A long driveway led up from its entrance gate to the main hotel lobby.

That very same afternoon we had our first meeting in the Colonel's office, a rather productive session. I was satisfied with the line of questions that indicated that we were rapidly getting on the same page.

Ernestina, his secretary, was a very effusive and attractive young lady, very voluble and gushing all over, except when it came to the English language; there it became a language of shrugs, with those dark, beautiful eyes hitting the ceiling or sky depending on where we stood, and lots of beautiful body language, and a beautiful body it was.

***

Late the next morning, I called the office to remind and confirm that we had a four o'clock meeting again that day. Ernestina was on the line in her usual gushing manner of which I understood absolutely nothing.

"Senorita Ernestina, ¿como esta? Soy Alex Kaufman, yo quiero confirmar la conferencia con el Coronel Hidalgo hoy a las 4 PM. ¿Esta bien?" I approached her in my best Pidgin Spanish:

" Miss Ernestina, how are you? I am Alex Kaufman, I wish to confirm the meeting with Colonel Hidalgo for four o'clock today."

"Oh, Señor Alex, El Coronel no esta en la oficina, El Coronel Hidalgo se fue a la guerra." She answered in a lilting voice, going from a sad regretful tone to one laden with great importance.

"Oh, Mr. Alex, the Colonel is not in the office. Colonel Hidalgo went to war."

"¿Fue a la Guerra? ¿Esta en Guerra? ¿A donde esta en Guerra?"

"He went to war? There is a war? Where is the war?" I replied in true astonishment.

"Aqui, en Quito Señor. ¿No escucha las bombas?"

"Here in Quito sir. Didn't you hear the bombs?"

"¿Bombas? No, no escucho las bombas. ¿Quando volvera el Coronel?"

"Bombs?" I repeated, "...no, I did not hear any bombs."

Then turning to the practical at hand, I asked "When will the colonel be back?"

"Oh, a mas tardar mañana," she assured me.

"Oh, tomorrow afternoon."

"¿A que hora? Posiblemente a las 4 PM?" I decided to press it a bit.

"At what time, is four o'clock possible?"

"Si, si, no hay problema. OK, Senŏnr Alex. Hasta mañana a las quatro," she came back assuring me again.

"Yes, yes, no problem, Mr. Alex. Tomorrow at four."

"Oh, grandioso hasta mañana!"

"Oh, That's great, I am happy. Till tomorrow."

This Pidgin English and Spanish conversation ended in a torrent of laughter and good cheer, while according to Ernestina a war was raging outside the door.

The road that passed the hotel was on an incline. The dilapidated trucks climbing and descending the hilly path day and night backfired constantly, thus it was impossible to discern between gunfire and backfire. Who could tell?

Since this particular day was shot, I decided to catch up on some work and go over the various presentation scenarios I planned to show the Colonel. I retired to the Hilton pool, a lovely grassy spot that overlooked the entrance and a section of the street, just to keep an eye on the war should it come passing by.

*****

Indeed, a couple of hours later, as I was dozing on my beach chair, I was startled by a sudden shrieking of breaks and lo and behold, the war must have come knocking. Three helmeted, dark green clad figures jumped off the military jeep and in quick-step came marching up the grassy hillock that extended to the gate below. Curiously I followed their movements and suddenly it seemed like they were heading straight at me, which indeed they were.

"Mr. Alex Kaufman, so nice to see you enjoying our country. It is an important war and we won!" A voice came from under a steel helmet topping a bemedaled chest.

"Huh?" I mustered a reply, and then I saw what looked to me like my colonel. "Colonel Hidalgo, so nice to see you again."

"Yes, yes, I just wanted to come by and tell you that we cannot meet today, I am very busy today with winning this war, but Ernestina will try to get in touch with you and we will meet tomorrow."

"Yes, yes I already talked to her, tomorrow at four."

"Well I am sorry that I cannot have dinner with you tonight, but we will do it tomorrow."

"I look forward to it. How is it going Colonel?"

He raised his thumb again, with the other hand flat on his chest, shook my hand, his two adjutants saluted and bowed and he said: "We are proud to win."

Never wanting to get involved in local politics, I gingerly replied, "So I see, I am glad you did and good luck to you, hasta mañana, my friend!"

**

Well, that gave me time to explore Quito and not stray into enemy territory perceived or real or wherever it was and not end up a prisoner of war. Off I went, traipsing the undulating streets to check out this charming city. I was especially taken by the old section of town, a gem from the colonial period. To no surprise I discovered that this section of town, together with Cracow in Poland - of all places - have been declared World Heritage sites, due to their outstanding and authentic state of preservation.

Quito is a very lively town, and it reflects the history of Ecuador and its struggle for independence from Spain. An Inca Empire before it fell to Spain, much of its vast lands were parceled off after independence to what is now Colombia. A small country in comparison to others on that continent, it is rich in agricultural resources, such as sugar, cocoa, coffee, bananas, shrimp and natural resources such as lumber, but of course its most important crop and most reliable source of its economy is oil.

The Pacific port of Guayaquil is where the revolution against Spain started and was led by Antonio Jose de Sucre. It is the largest and wealthiest city in Ecuador, a major oil port as well as the gateway to the Galapagos Islands. Ecuador has a plethora of flora and fauna species not easily found anywhere.

To my surprise, the coin of the realm, so to say, was the US dollar, although the Sucre was used. I liked the place very much, it was friendly, easy to understand, and a sort of a place you can get your arms around. And the food, definitely something to write home about, if I'd only remember what it was; delicious is all I can attest to.

***

Next day, at four in the afternoon I arrived at the Colonel's office. He welcomed me, rubbing his hands, and calling out, "OK it worked, it all worked out, we won!"

There was no trace of army paraphernalia nor steel helmets in sight. It was all business. He was again clad in a white shirt. I felt compelled to compliment Ernestina on her accurate clairvoyance that the war would be over by four in the afternoon, as indeed it was. We sat down to conduct our business in an atmosphere of peace. I could not help wondering what my Colonel could do in the Middle East. But then I dismissed the thought before it developed further. Things were back to normal, whatever the normal was. Or were they?

Tehran

Gorba was the nicest guy you would want to meet. He just could not be more helpful and all was done with good cheer. A real good companion who knew where things were and where the dogs were buried - the important dogs, that is. From a carpet to a minister, he would produce them. If you needed a carpet, an entire cartful of carpets, including the constantly-bowing dealer, they would appear right in front of your door and at prices pre-approved by Gorba. You needed to see a minister and have an extra door opened? Gorba was there, fulfilling the task with aplomb and enthusiasm. You needed to meet an important prince from across the straits in Saudi Arabia? Gorba made the connection. A live wire if there ever was one.

Manucher Gorbanifar, or Gorba as everyone called him for short, was from Isfahan, where he worked as a tour guide on sightseeing buses and where his father supposedly headed the local SAVAK, the Shah's secret police, the important pillar that held up the throne and through which the Shah maintained and exercised his power. Gorba knew everybody, and the ones he did not know he made them believe that he knew them. "What a guy" was the best way one could describe him. He was smart in the ways of human manipulation and traded on his connections, perceived and real. He knew how to sell himself and specialized in foreigners, strangers to the ways of Iran. He worked his capital and parleyed it into becoming a central figure in the Iran-Contra affair.

I met Gorba when he served as a sort of official gofer in the offices of Yadolla Shabazi, a recent Deputy Prime Minister in the Shah's government, who had retired to devote himself, unhindered, to the art of making money, which the foreigners heaped on him. Shabazi graciously let me use his offices during my stay in Teheran. I was there to advise and sell a factory-made housing system that I helped design. The prospective customers for it were his former colleagues in the government who headed the vast Ministries of Oil and the Interior, the mayor of Tehran, and the generals in charge of the Air Force, the Navy, and the Army, as well as the services such as the SAVAK and also the Red Crescent, the Iranian Red Cross. They all were in need of immediate housing. That's where we were supposed to come in.

I was somewhat familiar with Iran from earlier visits and consulting work I had done for Iran Air and its president, General Khatemi, as well as his deputy directors. They were excellent and wise people, who frequently came to New York, thus affording me the chance to reciprocate in some measure the generous hospitality they showed me in Tehran. Later, after the Khomeni takeover, I learned that General Khatemi, a Baha'i, was shot point-blank when he opened the door to his house, as was his wife. It greatly saddened me.

Iran, of course, is a fascinating place due to its rich past. The Persian Empire was one of the most enlightened of ancient empires. It was huge and spread from the Mediterranean to the Indian Ocean, encompassing an incredible array of tribes, nations, and religions. The Empire's emphasis was tax collection. To assure efficient transfers, it developed a fast relay system of riders who brought the money back to the royal seat at Persepolis. So long as taxes were paid, the people of the realm were free to worship any god they wished and exercise any religion, with no restraints imposed.

And then there was Persepolis, a true marvel. An incredible complex of structures and art, somewhat akin to the Forum Romanum. A majestic place, a delight, and an unexpected surprise to some visitors.

I was invited to Iran to offer a most efficient and innovative method of building houses, considering the lack of certain materials and skilled labor and the urgent need to satisfy demand. In my exhibit design work, I had developed techniques that required the set up of large and complex structures within hours, then dismantling them in about the same time and shipping them back out. My method here took into consideration all these elements and, most importantly, that the work would be done in remote areas, in a totally self-sufficient manner, without the availability of heavy construction equipment and with no existing instant supply lines.

Elements were made in the U.S. and designed to fit standard overseas shipping containers, which were to be loaded on RO-RO ships, or Roll On-Roll Off vessels, where containers were parked on chassis that were hitched on to tractors that simply drove the loads off the ship. This enabled the RO-RO ship to dock at any port, eliminating the requirement for gantries and other mechanical facilities at the port.

The big problem to overcome in those heady days was to get an unloading berth at the port. Upon arrival of a ship, it needed a secured spot to dock without waiting. Enter our former deputy prime minister Shabazi. It was his specialty, for a very hefty fee. He was very good at it. To fully appreciate this recurring daily feat and agree to the "smooth docking" fee he charged, all one had to do was to scan the horizon as far as the eye could see and watch the hundreds of ships languishing offshore, bobbing in the water with their cargo for months.

The lobby and restaurant of the Intercontinental Hotel in Tehran was busy and humming almost twenty-four hours a day, seven days a week. Salesmen, engineers, and peddlers from all corners of the world were parked there, in-between their appointment calls. We were competing with one another. It was interesting to watch how people were leaning back on two legs of their chairs, feigning reading documents when, in fact, they were eavesdropping on the next table, hoping to get some helpful information.

But the crown belonged to the fax guy. For fifty dollars and up, depending on the quality and quantity, one could buy the competition's confidential fax messages, cost estimates, and all the pertinent information. The fax office was on a side corridor, with a window and small counter right next to the men's room. That little, insignificant corridor was jam-packed at all hours. In addition to the payoffs, many worked on currying favor with the fax guy by bringing him trays of dinner, drinks, steaks, lobster - anything expensive and impressive. It was not unusual to observe three dinner trays stacked up at his window. No fax was immune, yet this was the only means of communication overseas to the home offices before the internet and e-mails.

"We are going on a picnic this Saturday," Yadolla informed me. Afterwards, we would go for dinner to the house of the head of the Red Crescent, way up north, next to the Caspian Sea. Indeed picnic baskets were lined up, loaded into our caravan of three cars and, after a two-hour ride or so, we spread out on a lovely meadow overlooking a verdant valley. The servants who followed us in the next car unloaded the baskets, set up the porcelain dishes and silverware on beautiful lace napkins and crystal decanters of wine and champagne. It was a movie set of a Victorian Picnic and I said so to Yadolla and his wife, who were relishing the appreciation. It was just something out of a dream - this was some picnic. No roughing it here.

We then drove on for another hour or so, and reached a villa on the crest of a hill. Recent rains had left this rural setting looking a bit muddy. We were welcomed by the owner, the Red Crescent boss, as well as an entourage of other guests, who all came out to greet us. As I stepped into the house, right out of nowhere a servant whooshed down, lay in front of my feet and cleaned my shoes, leaving them in better shape than they were when I had bought them.

The host invited us all for a drive, wanting to show me the beauty of the seaside. In our drive, we passed scenically beautiful sections and I was struck by one thing - I did not see any boats, yet we were in an ideal sea resort area.

"No boats?" I asked. "Do you have a boat, sir?" I inquired of our host. I got some evasive answers and did not want to press the point. On the way back to Tehran, late that night, Gorba explained:

"People here don't need boats. No reason to have a boat. On the other side is Russia."

"Excuse me. I am talking pleasure boats, not warships. Boats people can rent or use on their own in marinas. I did not see any marinas."

"Well, the Shah does not want people to go all over the place and leave Iran without him knowing. Also, there are spies, and there are the Kurds. You know what? It's better without boats."

"That's what it looks like, but it looks funny, a whole big sea and I haven't seen one boat in it yet."

I flew down one day to check out the ports of Bandar Shapur, Khoram Shah, and Bandar Abbas. I arrived at the first port in the evening. It was dark when we sat down at a sea-side restaurant for dinner. As we looked out towards the sea, my first question was, "Where is the sea?"

In front of us, I saw what looked like to me a lit-up city with flickering lights to the far end.

"You are looking at it," I was told with a big laugh. "What you see are ships at anchor waiting to dock and unload."

It was a truly amazing sight and what was more amazing was that our patron Shabazi could pick and choose the ship he wanted out of the line and bring it to shore. Yadolla Shabazi made out very well with bringing in the ships, turning them around, and repeating this like clockwork.

***

We were scheduled to meet with the Minister of Oil, probably the most important minister in the Shah's government. He was the guy with his hand on the spigot, the liquid money machine that made the world pay attention to this Shah and his people. I wonder what would have happened if all they had had in Iran was their pistachios and caviar. Mind you, dear reader, those are very good, too. Just not as good as oil.

The Ministry was a large grey stone and glass building, set back from the road with a plaza in front of it. It sat on a sort of a rise, reachable by climbing a flight of steps up to it. Entering the minister's office on the top floor, there were carpets all over, covering the floor, one on top of another, huge ones and with the most beautiful colors and designs. I had never seen carpets of such size. The minister was a trim guy, with an agitated speech pattern. We then sat down, the minister, Yadolla, and I, after having gone through the pleasantries of how we were, which none of us gave a hoot about. The minister took off his jacket, and, out of nowhere a servant appeared and then disappeared with his jacket as quickly as he had come. The minister leaned back on his swivel chair and proceeded to utter a barrage directed at me. He started in English and, as he picked up speed, switched to Persian.

"My dear Mr. Kaufman," he said, "…you come here to pick up the gold off our streets. You all do that. Do you think we will just stand by and let you do it? You Americans only come for the money. Money, money."

"Well sir, I hear what you are saying…."

"Am I wrong!? Did I say one thing that's wrong!?" he interrupted me, not letting me finish my sentence. He was now almost screaming, his face contorted, full of venom, making an effort to get it out. Something was clearly bugging him. Maybe his lunch did not agree with him. Or, I start thinking, he could be in need of a doctor.

"No, sir. I can only speak for myself. I have had a chance to walk the streets of Tehran, your beautiful city. I strolled down Elizabeth Boulevard and Takhte Jamjid and I must say sir, I did not see one piece of gold shimmer on the street. I must commend the city. It is extremely clean, nothing to be found on the streets."

Yadolla related it to the minister and patted him on his knee, in an attempt to cool him down.

"Is that what you said?" he now said in English, throwing me fierce look.

"I fully trust the Deputy Prime Minister's translation to you, sir."

"Well, the oil money stays here, nothing for you to take to America."

"Thank you, sir," I replied and started to get up. 'No it won't go to America. It'll go to Switzerland instead to your account there,' I say to myself. I shook his hand and got ready to leave.

"I will work out the cost numbers with Shabazi," he informed me, in an entirely different tone, out of the blue or out of a puddle of oil, as if we had come to an agreement and everything he had said before was just a piece of advertising. It probably was.

The meeting may possibly have been recorded or observed in some manner. It was a charade that he put on, so as to present a squeaky-clean record in a sea of corruption. It was so transparent. Not the type of transparency that might have saved the regime, but a convoluted, engineered one.

Waiting for us below, Gorba was leaning on the car as we came down.

"How'd it go, do you think?" he asked, trying to curb his curiosity.

"It didn't go. Nothing went. The guy up there believes that I came here to pick up the gold off the sidewalks. He didn't really want to listen to me, so I don't believe there's a 'go.'"

"No, no, there will be, you'll see. It will go big. Did he talk tough?"

"The toughest."

"Good!" Gorba rubbed his hands and his face was all smiles. "Then we got it, we got a deal, you made out good."

"I love you Gorba," I said, cementing the bond between us.

Yadolla just looked at him knowingly.

***

One afternoon I went on a walk about town and strolled down Takhte Jamshid, a main shopping street replete with stores and cafes. Suddenly, sirens blared and policemen came running from all sides of the street, shouting for everyone to face the walls of the buildings, not to look towards the road, and forced the traffic to pull over and stop along the curb. At that instant, a caravan of cars came whizzing by at high speed. It was the Shah and his entourage on an outing. Facing a big shop window, I could follow this man-made commotion and watched the Rolls Royces go by. I couldn't help thinking that the Shah's days were numbered. The more time I spent in this place, the more this feeling grew. Now if I could smell it after just a few days here, what about this Shah and his sense of smell?

***

Back in Shabazi's office, he showered me with compliments about our meeting with the minister.

"The minster likes you. You did very well there."

"I did? Or are you buttering me up?"

"No butter, nothing, but we will go to south Tehran this afternoon and you will explain to the people, the local housing committee, how we will build more houses for them with your superior method that that will give them insulation summer and winter and more solid homes."

"Is this a political job in support of the government?"

"It's in support of the Shah, a great opportunity."

As we arrived in chauffeur-driven cars, we stepped out next to a crowd of locals assembled in the middle of the street and taking up the entire width of the road from left to right. For a minute, I thought this was a demonstration, but the people were stationery, no placards and no signs. Someone produced a card table and placed it in the middle of the street, chairs appeared, and the leaders and our group of five all sat down.

Gorba opened the convocation and suddenly the crowd pushed forward, overturning the table and the chairs and in no time yelling and screaming obscenities at the Shah and throwing bricks. I was observing this while trying to shield myself from the flying brick missiles and other flying debris. Where did these bricks come from? I didn't see any when we arrived. A closer look revealed the mystery - they were tearing them out of the walls. The mayhem turned into a full-fledged anti-Shah protest, with lots of spitting after the mention of his name, shoes flying in the air and fists being waved at us.

"Get into the cars, get in!" Gorba shouted, collecting us. The cars took off at high speed with some of the doors still open.

"Gorba, what was this all about?"

"They no good, they are anti–Shah people. The houses you saw there…the Shah built those for them for free, but they do not like them. They say the houses are shit."

"You mean the brick apartment houses, like we have in our low-income areas in our cities back home?"

"Yes, and the Shah was very generous. But that's not good enough for these people. They cried that the Shah should live in them, that they'll bury him in there, that his housing makes his friends rich while they suffer the cold in the winter, no repairs, bad construction."

"So that's why they started taking it apart brick by brick and throwing them at us?"

"How'd you know?" Gorba asked, surprised.

"I was there, remember?"

South Tehran was a working-class area with lots of poor, all within eyesight of the rich and the ones who were getting richer. It was highly religious and a Khomeini stronghold. It was probably the only place in Tehran, at that time, where the Shah was openly vilified. It seemed that neither the SAVAK nor the police were keen to go in there.

This can't last, I thought, referring to the Shah's rule. You force your people to look away when you drive through their streets? A very peculiar relationship with one's subjects. In South Tehran, it was very clear that this Shah was not going to last long. I saw murder in these people's eyes, an impatient murderous look.

***

Shabazi invited me to a series of dinners in his and his friends' houses. The people were lovely, very hospitable; the food was the best, local and imported, and good conversation. The members of these groups were wealthy, of course, and belonged to the elite of the country and were all foreign-educated, speaking a multitude of languages. They were businessmen, bankers, lawyers, doctors, and academics. These were very interesting and enjoyable evenings. I noticed one thing - they all had a plethora of servants taking care of everything in the house and assuring the comfort of the guests. However, I never met any children. None were ever to be seen.

"Where are the children?" I asked.

"In school," I was told.

"But it is ten in the evening now, surely they must be back?"

I was met with laughter.

"Where is this school?" I kept on.

"In Switzerland, in England, in France, some in Germany, some in the Netherlands, and some are in medical school in the United States."

"But what about the young ones, the teens and younger?"

"Boarding schools. Didn't you go to one?"

I guess that explained it. The wealthy, pro-Shah Iranians shipped their kids out, as soon as they could walk.

***

Gorba arranged an evening outing. Joining us would be his good friend Samir, who was currently managing a Saudi prince's business affairs and was very interested in putting in a large order for our housing system. Samir was a very gentle fellow, civilized, and a scion to a large and prominent Lebanese Christian family in Beirut. Their Khayat publishing house and book stores were famous throughout the region. Samir had escaped the Lebanese Civil War, and landed in Saudi Arabia, where he lent his business acumen to a local prince. Samir was a charming, highly intelligent fellow, an excellent conversationalist, very likable, and a man of the world. His wife was American from California, and they had two kids.

Gorba said that in tonight's outing we would be accompanied by two young ladies and would be going to a sort of cabaret/nightclub.

At the appointed time, two young ladies showed up, accompanied by an old lady in a jihab and long colorful kaftan, an eagle-eyed chaperon. We all sat around the table, while all kinds of hors d'œuvre type food dishes were brought in. The stony-faced chaperon did not say a word. She sat almost motionless, except that from time to time she would energetically chew on the foods in front of her. After about two hours, she pulled out an orange and silently started peeling it. She created an artistic pattern of the shape of the rinds and of the orange. Really a piece of art. Gorba complimented her, nodded and smiled. She kept peeling, never changing her mien. She did not smile nor frown, she just sat there and peeled.

"Tomorrow is your really big day. We are going to the Air Force," Gorba said to me.

"Are we going to fly somewhere?"

"No," he chuckled. "We are going to see General Khatomi, the commander of all the planes."

"Is he going to buy houses?"

"And how! More houses than you've ever seen."

"What about the other Generals, are we going to see them sometime, too?"

"Of course, we are arranging it."

"Why not get them altogether, all the Generals, and make a dinner for them? Then we can hit them all at once."

"Impossible, cannot be done. No more than two Generals are allowed to meet at one time in one place and they've got to tell the Shah before the meet. The Shah's orders."

"What? Why?"

"You ever heard of coups? How do you think coups happen? Generals meeting and plotting. The Shah does not like this. So, no meeting together of more than two Generals. You want to talk, talk so the Shah can hear it, too. That's the law."

Again I asked myself, how on earth can this Shah last? If this is not the writing on the wall, what is? They had writings on the walls in this same area a millennia ago. The Shah had never read about it nor was he reading it now. I recognized that his demise was only a matter of time. A short time, it seemed to me. Sometimes you go outside and you can feel a storm coming. That's what it felt like to me. I felt I ought to hurry and finish my business and get out of there.

A new singer came on, belting out the same song, it seemed, as all the others before her. Samir and I smoked our hookahs - called nargilas - and listened to Gorba, nodding our heads. I contemplated whether I should go with Samir the following week to Saudi Arabia.

***

"Let's go!" Yadolla urges, "No sense being late."

Since when is punctuality a factor in this country? But I kept quiet and my thoughts to myself. As we were about to enter the road, we were faced with a huge traffic jam. It felt like home, and it sure looked like the Long Island Expressway. Nothing moved, it all just stood there. Our cabby drove on the sidewalk, chasing down people at seventy miles per hour, scattering pedestrians and possibly leaving some road kill behind.

"Can you do that? Just drive down a sidewalk?"

"Well," he reasoned, "...you are not allowed to make a U-turn here."

"Well, In that case, it makes sense. You are one good driver."

It is rather educational to always get a glimpse of the native logic.

This time, we were in the north of Tehran. It was a much better neighborhood, modern, affluent, and leafy. No one demonstrating here. We pulled up at the headquarters of the Iranian Air Force. It was a nicely laid-out campus and we were led straight to the General's office.

As we entered, we were confronted by a long, rectangular space. The floor was covered with what seemed to me like mandatory layers of carpet. On both sides, long rows of chairs were lined up, occupied by lines of bemedaled, sash-clad officers. At the end of this long hall, which was easily seventy-five to a hundred feet in length, was a desk, positioned across it, like a road block. Behind it, the general was ensconced. The desk, too, was surrounded by chairs, some left open for visitors, others with more officers, occupying themselves with lists, writing things down and keeping busy. The long low-slung cabinet behind the desk was loaded with airplane models of all sizes and shapes. And further behind that was a large map of the world. As we approached and came closer to the General, it struck me how much he resembled Mel Brooks - in height, in tone, and in facial features and expressions. That was eerie. 'It can't be that this General Khatomi is a relative of Brooks,' I thought to myself. The general got off his chair and, bent forward, as if he was being weighted down by his ample collection of medals pinned to his chest, stretched out his arm in greeting.

After reviewing a few designs together with some of his aides he called over, we got down to the business of possibly ordering these structures for his pilots and their families.

We agreed on all major points, including cost. One more item I needed to ascertain.

"General, sir," I asked him, "...when it comes to toilets, which is your preference? We have European toilets, the chair height style, and we have oriental toilets, the squatting type."

Now he got excited. He put his cigar down, cleared his throat and came out from behind his desk, walked around it and came facing me, while buttoning up his tunic,

"Mr. Kaufman," he started, "…my pilots are the cream of the crop, the best! No, wait a minute, the very best!"

"Yes, sir, of course," I supported his statement.

He raised his hand in a stop motion, and then continued:

"You see Mr. Kaufman, we are spending more than a million dollars on each pilot to train him to fly like a European, to dress like a European, and to eat like Europeans, and so they may as well shit like Europeans. No oriental toilets, and that's final."

"Yes, sir, General."

I had to admit, the general had a point.

***

A few days later, I got a note hand-delivered by an Air Force officer – the General invited me to fly with him to a base on the Persian Gulf. He had taken a liking to me, this Mel Brooks doppelgänger.

We were to take off the following Thursday and that morning I was promptly picked up for an eleven o'clock AM flight. We whooshed down and the general seemed to be a pretty good pilot. I saw Isfahan and Shiraz from the air and he made a short loop over Persepolis, the fantastic ancient ruins which I had visited before and thought that they rivaled the Forum Romanum in Rome. After about a two hour flight, fields of parked aircraft came into view.

Upon landing we were whisked away by waiting jeeps and driven to the parked fighters. Accompanied by the local commander and a coterie of officers we walked around the planes and the general kicked a few tires. I suddenly noticed that the planes were all covered with a layer of fine desert sand. One could draw pictures on them by running a finger on the metal. 'They sure could use a good dusting,' I thought.

"It looks like they need a dusting or need to take off and fly somewhere," I said to the general.

"No, no, these are the most expensive planes in the world, the most advanced, I cannot tell you what's in them, but trust me," and he held his hands over his heart, "…they are very, very expensive and we leave them covered with the sand film, to test how well the preservation works and how effective the camouflage is. We monitor it all the time."

An intriguing explanation, I thought, and never a word about flying these graceful, exciting, sand-covered machines.

As I listened to the general and scanned the vast expanse of desert, covered with rows upon rows of brown-yellow sand-silhouetted fighter planes, all covered with the thin layers of desert sand, I had to admit that the general had a point. I know of archeological excavations unearthing thousand-year old mosaics and frescoes in pristine condition because they were covered with sand that preserved them for millenniums.

One thing was clear, the Shah, our ally at the time, was a very good ally. He only bought the best for his military; money was no object. He also provided work for our plane builders. Who was complaining? At the end of our tour, we flew back north to Tehran, over a brown-yellow wide-open landscape until we hit the congested area of Tehran.

Admittedly, it was a very educational trip.

***

The General was a very generous an amiable host. He pointed out some areas on his map where we would put the houses and then we flew back to Tehran, a distance of about seven hundred miles north. Upon parting, the General promised, that next time, he personally would fly me to another site in his personal fighter.

A short time later, I learned that the General, piloting his own plane, flew into a mountain and crashed. He was a nice general and boy, was I lucky.

Guard Shift

Midnight till six. The guy you are relieving is already out, rubbing his eyes, mumbling, "Watch it, there's stuff out there." As you get settled in the outpost and look out, your eyes slowly absorb the landscape you are supposed to watch, or do they? At first, it is all one big dark blob, no moon. Then shapes appear, igniting your imagination. Looks like a bush, could be a crouching figure. You turn your head and come back again and now it looks like two crouching bushes next to each other. You bend down to fish out your canteen from the knapsack to wet your dry throat and, getting back up, you scan the site again. Now it looks like one bush is gone. Has it moved? Is this rounded thing on it a head? Are you hallucinating? You close your eyes, then open them again. You bring your hand up to your face and with your thumb and index finger you pry your eyes open, holding them open as wide as possible. Like when taking eye drops. No sound from out there, or is there? Is it the wind? So what was it that you just heard? Yeah, the bush has moved; it is no longer there, and there is another shape there now, more squarish -

was it there before? "Idiot," you say to yourself, it surely depends on the angle from which you are viewing it. But you are not altogether sure it was a bush, although you'd like to believe it was. And what was that square thing? Did it just move? When you are visually inclined, there is no limit to what you can make out with perceived bushes you see in the dark. It's a bit like looking at the clouds, where some people can discern chariots or horses, or someone who can discern a cloud that looks exactly like Mr. Lifshitz, your old first grade teacher.

All this looking out starts dulling your senses. Your eyelids come down and you catch yourself sleeping. Did you sleep? Only way to prevent it is to eat. So you fish out the chicken leg, the oranges, the bread, and the candy bar. Then, you compare your food supply to the hours left and hope that it will last. At least you have something to worry about now - that should keep your eyes open.

Five-thirty in the morning. Finally. A stillness lies over the terrain like at no other time of the day. You can call out to the other side, three miles across, and get a reply. Sometimes a shouting conversation ensued, replete with choice curses. Calls like "Ya Ahmed!" Which is answered with a throaty "Ei -Wah, you Jewish dog!" And not necessarily by one named Ahmed. This is then followed by the first question of the day, sailing across the terrain: "Why is your ass red?" To which he would reply with an angry barrage of small arms fire. It happens every day: same question, same answer. Except for revealing the shooter's position, there was not much else to those silly encounters.

'Keep it quiet,' you think to yourself, '...let Ahmed sleep late. Another thirty minutes and you will be done and will be relieved. Why leave the outpost under a hail of bullets and have to wait till Ahmed gets tired of shooting? You want to get back to your bunk and breakfast.'

The early light is always entrancing. The line of light on the horizon from the rising sun solidly confirms that the night is over and a bright day is coming up in minutes. You just can't tear your eyes away from it - within a few minutes everything changes. A moment of awe overcomes you quickly, and for just a second you say to yourself that you are a man of nineteen, a soldier with his feet solidly on the ground and not given to soft, sentimental thoughts. Yet suddenly, you feel very small, the rapidly emerging dawn speaks to you in silence. This is big, you admit - it's all encompassing. It transcends everything around you. Its majestic size and beauty mocks everything you regard as so important. It pays no attention to them. It convinces you how miniscule, small, tiny, and insignificant you are in the scheme of things. If we believe that God created the world in six days, this was a good beginning - every morning, with all the enticement to do the next day's work, to check if what was done the day before worked, and to finish the job at hand. I am rising now, the sun pronounces with its sheer awesome presence, and I will be up there to stay and I will provide you with a new, bright day. And you, what are you going to make of this new day?

A lovely, inviting landscape. Hard to believe that less than an hour ago it was a scary, threatening mass, emanating danger, putting you on edge. Look at it, what a sight, an idyllic movie set, constantly changing to richer hues as the sun progresses upwards. Painted in soft brush strokes, with a rich palette. A cool, gentle breeze hovers over the heat, preparing to rise and soon envelop all. You can literally see the world change in front of you in slow motion, until the sun fully bursts through with a crescendo of light and color and warmth. Suddenly, you feel less threatened, even cocky. You know it's false, but you like to believe it; it's like a return for a moment to normal life. The same sun that shines on the outpost shines a few thousand miles away in other lands, on people having breakfast, kids rushing to school, trains and buses and cars filling up the streets, ferrying people to their normal daily endeavors. You keep looking back on your way off the outpost, slowing down as you walk. Impatient calls from the squad urge you on. You just want to savor the beautiful view. You want to inhale it. It makes you stop and look and absorb and turn with every other step, like you do not want to miss a minute of it, despite the fact that you counted the hours and minutes all night, waiting to get out of there.

It is nothing short of enthralling to see the terrain transformed into a friendlier, guileless landscape. It's like nature playing peek-a-boo. Still, it is a deceiving landscape. Where are the bushes you saw at night? There are no bushes at all out there. So what was it you saw? Looks peaceful, but who knows how many traps would await you there? Does daylight make you less alert? Could sympathizing with the lovely landscape make you lose your suspicion and alertness? On second thought, the threatening landscape shrouded in the dark of the night was suddenly more comfortable - it was hostile and at least you knew where you stood. You were prepared, tense and focused on watching every movement, sound, and the slightest noise, real and imagined. There was no room to feel relaxed, to love the landscape.

You were told to try to differentiate between hostiles and civilians - easier said than done if they all look the same. But what they forgot to mention was differentiating between animals and people. There is a whole world of nocturnal animals roaming and slithering around, mainly jackals, in addition to the occasional donkey, cow, and goats coming by. They could scare the dickens out of you. Scanning with the binoculars in the morning, there are always some animal casualties laying out there. On a hot day, with the sun relentlessly beating down, the waft of their rotting odor reaches the outpost. After a while, it becomes the underlying odor of the place.

When you get back to your bunk, a tremendous tiredness, rarely experienced before, overcomes you and you wonder why. You were practically sitting all night, doing nothing, just watching a sliver of land, so what makes you so washed-out tired? It takes some time to realize that this little six-hour task strained every nerve in your body, tensed every muscle, put every fiber on concentrated alert, and took every ounce of energy. Furthermore, it pumped it all up with trepidation, not counting the sporadic surges of your body's alertness from zero to the max and then shutting it down again when you realized that it was nothing. And there was the focusing - that really caused a headache. You don't believe your eyes have ever worked with such intensity, trying to discern a figure in the dark, follow its imaginary movement and, when it does indeed move, having all your senses explode all at once and having the brain get feverishly into the act at such a high pitch. When it turns out that there was nothing out there, your motor shuts off and it all drains out. Lucky, and stiff. But it's quiet, so you can relax a bit. Nothing happened. Back to square one and looking at the watch. As if looking at it made the time go faster. So what was the question? Why are you so tired from sitting around and doing nothing?

Wake up at lunchtime. The good stuff is gone by now. The midday shift ate an hour ago. It's like the locusts came through. But you feel good, refreshed, got nothing to do till midnight. This, too, can get you pretty tired. A different tired. Wish there was a beach here. Spotting bikinis beats spotting bushes. It's OK, keep dreaming.

Is Rommel Coming?

Growing up in the forties in the then Palestine, on the fringes of the Middle East and North African battles in World War II, was exciting if you were a kid.

Three years prior, from 1936 and running straight into the outbreak of the war was the so-called Arab Revolt. There was no ebb in emergency situations, blasting newspaper headlines, shootings, bombings and killings. So we were conditioned to the state of affairs, not really having experienced a lot of peace and tranquility in our short lives. Of course there was no comparison to had we remained in Europe.

Yet, we had ceaseless strife, and intercity travel was by bus with protective steel mesh on the windows defending against stone throwers. The economy? What economy? One barely made a living, and the trick was to go to the open air market or souk in the evening when the merchants and peddlers broke down their stands and just wanted to get rid of the day's remnants, offering ridiculous prices so long as the shopper would take it away. Going down with my father who by now sported a double hernia, my six-year-old muscles were strained to the limit in hauling the day's loot home.

Buildings were sparsely occupied, standing empty along long stretches of streets, and as soon as the so called 'Arab Revolt' subsided at the start of World War II, the Italian Air Force started to visit the city and leave their bomb droppings, just adding their share to the anxieties embedded in the populace. Soon this was overtaken by a yet bigger anxiety, a whole different anxiety, that is, once someone establishes how many anxieties there are. This new anxiety was all consuming. Daily, people checked out the map of North Africa displayed on Allenby, the main shopping street of Tel Aviv where practically every store displayed a map of North Africa, pasted to the inside of their windows, showing Rommel's progress in the direction of Alexandria, Cairo, the Suez Canal and up to Tel Aviv, some even displayed estimated times of his arrival.

However, come to think of it, we kids did our thing. We had a good time. We played basketball on the school's hoops with an old, frayed tennis ball, which got lost sometimes into the depths of the open top steel pipe that held up the boards.

I never participated in school trips; I did not dare to even ask for it. I knew there was no money, period. But we were happy, so at least it seemed to me. We were busy and during the summer vacation we played outdoors from morning till when the moon stood high in the sky. We even played a game akin to baseball called 'Hakafot,' with minor different rules, but basically followed the same pattern as baseball. Equipment? No one ever mentioned it; we had sawed-off broom handles and the ubiquitous fraying tennis ball. We were prolific consumers and got the very maximum out of these balls until the ball literally died. Ever see a ball die? You should have been there. There was no time to mourn it - 'find a new ball' was the prevailing need.

***

Before the heavy onset of the war, there was Abyssinia or Ethiopia. Mussolini defeated the arrow and lance-wielding army of Heile Selassie and one day, the emperor showed up in Tel Aviv, the first station of his exile. Our family welcomed him, too. He added much needed money to our sparse income. How? Connections. Tel Aviv had a ballroom dance school on Ben Yehuda street, run by Hans Gut. His mother befriended mine and, to make a short story shorter, Hans Gut was commissioned by the British to handle a royal reception for the emperor, the Lion of Judah, at the San Remo hotel on the Tel Aviv seafront. It was a black-tie affair and my father was employed in the coat room and was provided with a tuxedo by Hans Gut. The cream of the local society attended as well as senior British government officials including the High Commissioner. My dad came home with a nice cache of earnings as well as bags of food, left over and distributed among the employees after closing. A short few years later, the whole thing repeated itself again, when General Alan Cunningham chased the Italians out of Ethiopia and met the emperor in Tel Aviv to accompany him back to Addis Ababa in triumph.

***

While the war was brewing and then raging outside, it never touched us except for sporadic air bombardments by the Italians from Rhodes and the Germans from a Vichy air base near Aleppo in Syria. Young men from the street were joining the British army, ending up in the Cyrenaican desert, first under generals Wavell, Cunningham, Alexander and Ritchie, then Auchinleck and finally Montgomery, who was brought in by Churchill. We monitored the series of generals in tandem with the Axis advance along the Libyan/Egyptian coastlines, and both kept changing all the time. The generals, who came and went and although they never knew it, had fans among us. Ritchie was a favorite, because he took his dog along to all the briefings and interviews. We were very much attuned to this, tearing ourselves away from our doings.

It was a glorious summer. We had time on our hands but had no means to favor the ice cream vendor who came by periodically. I, at least, was in dire need of money. To earn extra money I got into the business of collecting horse and mule droppings, occasionally also a camel's that for sure beat the droppings on Tel Aviv the Italian air force left behind. I loaded it all into my wheelbarrow and then sold it to the people down the street who were tending Victory gardens and growing vegetables. One day, wheeling my half-full wheelbarrow along, the air sirens went on, with every one seeking refuge in the makeshift air raid shelters. Houses at that time in Tel Aviv had no basements. Shelters usually consisted of an inside corridor, not exposed to windows, on the first ground floor apartment, one could reach. Well I followed into such a shelter and took my loaded wheelbarrow with me and nested it next to me at the end of the corridor. I wasn't going to risk having Lieberman, a kid, one of three brothers, notorious for stealing other people's drop- pings, get hold of my cart, had I left it outside. The corridor was full of people, mostly sitting on available hassocks. At first everything was normal in the shelter on a sweltering summer afternoon. People were fanning themselves with newspapers and anything flat that could generate some needed air. After a while, nostrils became active until they discovered my pile of loot. While the alarm was on and the sound of airplane motors was discernible I could stay, but had to wheel my barrow outside the corridor. However, as soon as the all-clear sounded, I was given friendly advice - not to show up with my goods, ever again.

***

We got a daily geography and history lesson following the BBC news and the maps that were displayed on Allenby of the North African campaign and calculating the day that Rommel would show up in Tel Aviv. For some reason, Marshall Graziani, the commander of the Italian Army in Libya, didn't worry anybody, but the arrival of Rommel gave a deep boost of lingering anxiety to everyone around us.

My uncle who, against the prevailing Nazi laws, left Germany with all his money that he smuggled out in loads of hollow brass curtain rods, and whom the Nazis honored with a Wanted Poster, rushed to change his surname to Hebrew, so the Germans, once in Tel Aviv, would fail to find him.

Yet, for us, times were exciting. Our games and plays were consuming our time, not leaving much for worrying about Rommel. However, we were all engaged in strategy and Alush was the chief strategist. He convinced us that he 'knew.' In very condescending tones he patiently explained to us as we bunched around him, so as not to lose any of the pearls of wisdom that were emanating from his mouth. He declared that this Rommel thing was all nonsense, Rommel would never make it to Tel Aviv; he had to cross the Suez Canal and the Red Sea for that.

"No, fellows, have you already forgotten Pharaoh's fate when he tried it? It'll never happen, it can't. Had that poor sucker Rommel read his Bible he would never have thought of attempting it."

We protested and reminded Alush that Rommel was a German, a no-good Nazi. In chorus we asked why he could be trusted not to cross the Canal?

"Because he is no dummy." This was according to Alush, who knew it from very reliable sources. What were these very reliable sources? We knew, but we never asked. Alush's parents ran a major fish store, everybody, house servants to high-ranking British Mandate and Jewish officials, to doctors and all kinds of people from the multitude of escapees from Europe, to Polish generals and the many who assembled in Palestine to regroup and join the fight again by being incorporated into the 8th Army - the Greeks, the Free French, Belgians, Poles, Australians, New Zealanders, you name them, they all patronized the fish store and Alush whispered that there were a whole slew of spies there too. Shivek, one of the bright ones in the lot, asked "Why in the fish store, do they all eat fish?"

Alush replied "You seen any steaks lately? There is no meat, where were you, didn't you see the rationing?"

Shivek, not giving up so easily, asked " ...and spies eat fish?"

"That's all they eat, my friend," Alush, firmly and knowingly pronounced.

So there we stood one night after supper at the usual time we always met to talk. Talk about what? Everything, especially the war. After that, we'd go to the German Templar cemetery at the other end of the large empty lot that belonged to the Mandate Survey Office and that was run by the British. Along the fence of the cemetery were thick growths of cactus that bore prickly pear fruit. They came in yellow, red and purple. The yellow were preferable, since the drip spots of the red and purple ones on shirts and pants would not come out in the washing. The yellow pears were more amenable. Those prickly pears were sold all summer by street vendors all over town, nesting on a bed of chopped ice and people paid good money for it. The German cemetery pears were fat, juicy and relatively easy to open without getting the tiny prickly thorns all over one's hand and fingers. So there we stood around talking, usually at the corner entrance to my house, at Kiryat Sefer 4, next to where all the bicycles were tied up.

Eliezer, a kid who lived across the street started by saying that the Germans were killing Jews in Europe. "They assemble them and shoot them and not only men, but women and children and they do so by the millions." We all looked at him in disbelief. People just don't go around shooting people like that, even if they're Germans. I mean, we knew Germans, they lived in their village Sarona only a few hundred feet away from the end of Kiryat Sefer Street. We went strolling in their village. Yes, they had swastika flags out on Sundays, I even knew a kid from there who once gave me an old bicycle he found while plowing. As soon as the war was declared, the British scooped up the entire village and shipped them to Australia as enemy aliens.

From then on, this talk repeated itself every night when we got together and every one came in with another version he heard somewhere, of the killings and of the plan the Germans had to kill all the Jews in the world. Well, now the monitoring of Rommel assumed a whole new dimension fraught with nervous tension and greater urgency.

"What do you guys think we should do?" I asked. Everyone of the gang suddenly got very quiet. Some gulped and Lieberman had this very panic stricken look on his face, his arrogance drained out of him and he became very nervous and cut out early, very much not his style. This was the first time we heard about of what became known as the Holocaust.

We now went down daily to Allenby Street, to the store windows and the display of maps. Rommel's advances were updated and constantly marked on the maps. We all started getting knots in our stomachs. We checked, we ran our fingers over the glass displaying the maps behind it with the red lined markings pointing in the easterly direction. Benghazi, Tripoli, Tobruk, Derna, Bardia, Mersah Matrukh, Sollum, Sidi Barani, El Aghelia, El Alamein, Alexandria, El Arish, the Canal --- and then, oh my God it is getting closer, too close! What are we going to do?

We were all boys, we were all students in the same school, we were orthodox, or were supposed to be, we all went to Bilu, and the girls went to Talpiot, three blocks away. We looked for people; we wanted more people around us. Some of the kids on our street had no desire to socialize with us. Some were not allowed to come out late at night. Others were congregating with their own kind somewhere else. We felt the need to talk to others, hear what they thought of doing, in case…the unspoken 'in case,' of Rommel walking down Allenby ahead of his murdering troops.

***

One early morning, it was summer and still dark out there, lorries, as the British called trucks, full of soldiers came up the street and disgorged hundreds of Tommies in battle gear. Within hours they pitched tents on the vast open Mandate's Survey Office lot, placed bricks denoting thoroughfares and pedestrian walks, painted them white, erected a field kitchen that as soon as the equipment stood up vertically, smells of food wafted from the smoke of cooking over the neighborhood. They drew water lines to the outdoor showers and in no time the battalion was settled and bivouacked.

We kept up our nightly gatherings. In order to reach the cemetery cactus perimeter to harvest our prickly pears, we had to cross the Survey Office lot, now a British Army camp. How were we going to do this? Lieberman, recovered from his Rommel panic attack, said "Tell them."

So we made up a delegation, our English was dismal. We appealed to teacher Meisel, our English teacher, and he wrote it out on the back of an exercise book, "Please let my students go through your camp to pick prickly pears and return the same way."

The next day we walked into the camp. The soldiers smiled at us and we spotted a sergeant. We did not know what he was, but he had three impressive V-shaped stripes with a gold metal crown in the middle of them, so we decided that this was the guy we were going to approach. We did and it worked. He read it, waved his hand and said something that did not sound like English at all. He had a very heavy accent of some type, but he was English, we assumed. Later, we found out that he was from London. Well, how much more English can you get?

***

The battalion stayed for months, it was later supplemented by Indian troops. Every morning at five o'clock sharp, they blew bugles, waking up the battalion and in the process, the whole of Kiryat Sefer Street.

Every night the question came up - what are we going to do when Rommel gets here? Well something was done. At that time, the British established, together with the local Jewish leadership, the Palmach units to act as a clandestine armed resistance, partisan unit to give Rommel as much trouble as possible. That's what Lidor, a kid who actually lived on a parallel street but was taken in by us, said. His uncle who was a

Hagana official told his parents. Among the group, there were some who did not want to believe that the Germans were shooting Jews. This resulted at times in very heated arguments, each faction asking the other for proof. At that time, there was none.

I had six cousins, they were all siblings and each one lived in a different Kibbutz, spread out all over the country from the east shore of the Sea of Galilee to the lower Negev. One, Eliyahu, a member of Kibbutz Yagur next to Haifa, became an early member of the Palmach and a contemporary of Moshe Dayan and a whole group consisting of these early recruits to the Palmach. I liked Eliyahu; my father used to be his baby sitter in Germany when he was called Ernst. Later, he became a recognized soccer player beating the Hitler Youth team in his Blue and White Maccabi uniform. Eliyahu used to stop by on Kiryat Sefer on his way to the Negev or Jerusalem on his various assignments. He liked my dad a lot. The British general Orde Wingate trained these guys in guerilla warfare. I could now talk about it and lead the conversation about what Rommel could expect once he would come up from Egypt. The fact that a trained unit would attempt to sabotage his every move, calmed us down. We gained confidence. Rumors about the Afrika Korps still spread some nervousness and soon strong suggestions for Rommel surfaced, advising that he better not come, unless he was looking for a final resting place. However, the nervousness remained. Jitters were embedded, throats became suddenly dry with fright, settled deep in our stomachs. It did not help either when we listened on the BBC to Hadj Amin al Husseini, the Mufti of Jerusalem, broadcasting from Nazi occupied Yugoslavia, that he would accompany Rommel to Palestine at the head of his German trained SS divisions.

***

With all that, times were busy for us. When school was over and we were in the almost three months of summer recess, we kept busy.

Except for the nightly meetings, I pursued my fertilizer collection business, did artwork, wrote for the newspaper, then I founded another newspaper and it must have been the only newspaper that changed its name on its masthead as soon as some exciting political situation came up, which I considered important for changing the paper's name in honor of the event and to commemorate it or the place of its occurrence. We were also busy playing ball, taking excursions, going to the beach and, of course, going downtown to check on Rommel.

We were in the middle of the war. In the Middle East, the British were busy protecting their oil resources in Iran and Iraq. A new threat came from Syria. The French Mandate holders of Syria and Lebanon went over to Vichy and Petain after the Germans occupied France. General Dentz, headquartered in Damascus, commanded the French forces loyal to Vichy. The Aleppo airport was occupied by the Luftwaffe which flew bombing sorties to Haifa's port and refineries and to Tel Aviv's Reading power station. Palestine, under British mandate, became a huge marshalling yard for the British forces in Egypt and Libya, commanded by a whole string of generals, who were hired and fired in rapid succession with finally Montgomery cobbling together his 8th Army at the Egyptian fly-infested village of El Alamein. This force could have been called a United Nations force, only the UN did not exist yet then. It was made up, as already mentioned, of detachments from every country Hitler conquered - Greeks, French, Poles, Dutch, Belgians and it was heavy on British empire troops - Indians, Senegalese, Kenyans, Burmese, Australians, New Zealanders and, of course British and over fifty thousand Palestinian Jewish volunteers, a huge number considering the size of the Jewish population of five hundred thousand in Palestine at the time. Palestine became the R&R hub for all these armies and a staging area for fighting the Africa Korps down in the desert. Wherever one went, one saw uniforms identified by their badges, naming their countries of origin.

The Australians stood out at once with their big floppy hats and their happy go-lucky demeanor. One day, I remember vividly, a group of possibly twenty-five Australians, coming out of a bar on Tel Aviv's main business street Allenby, by the way named after the British general who conquered Palestine from the Turks in WWI. As they strolled down the street, they spotted a group of mothers carrying their babies on their arms followed by toddlers as they were walking along. On Allenby there was this big pram store, directly across the street from the Eckmann department store and next to the Flaumenhaft restaurant, offering baby and toddler carriages and strollers. With great fanfare and laughter, the Aussies guided the women into the pram store, bought carriages for all the babies and toddlers after conducting a count, lined them up on the street, held off the traffic and placed the kids in the prams and strollers. The young mothers were elated. Once the babies were all settled in their new carriages they organized a parade and marched them down the street. Harmonicas appeared and they started playing their music and further locomoting the march by a robust rendition of Waltzing Matilda. The whole procession was a sight to see, the mothers were at first taken aback and then happily surprised. The entire stretch of Allenby, a rushing and hustling section, suddenly broke out in cheers, laughter never heard before and waves of applause. Women went up to the soldiers and kissed them. Talking about lifting spirits? Lingering concerns about Rommel? This was a contagious euphoria. It just made everyone around happy. Yet the Australians seemed to have had the best time of all.

They loved the Kibbutz farms and the people there. There, they were at home. Off came their shirts and they dug into farm chores with relish. They loved the girls with their very short khaki pants, and their laughter echoed from the cow sheds, the barns and wherever they were. Being mostly farm boys, there was no tractor, plow or horse they didn't like and could not resist on jumping on and putting it to work.

They were quick studies when it came to dancing the Hora till the wee hours. Due to a lack of liquor, they were guzzling orange juice, a real novelty, singing and smoking and then singing some more and drinking more orange juice.

There was no prohibition against liquor, Kibbutznicks just did not have it and were not used to drinking hard liquor.

***

In Libya and Egypt it developed into a back and forth situation. One side would attack and prevail for a short time till the next counter attack came on. This repeated itself for some time. It seemed to all that Rommel was thwarted and was definitely not going to show up in Tel Aviv. A big sigh of relief ensued, where you could literally hear the collective exhalation.

In the North, together with the newly formed Palmach, the British defeated the Vichy forces, took General Dentz prisoner, brought him to Jerusalem and that ended the threat from Syria. The Luftwaffe too was gone from Aleppo, another averted threat. Both Rommel and Montgomery became stars of the war. They earned their fame in Libya and a lasting fame it is.

Montgomery was now chasing Rommel away from us and then one day, in the vicinity of one of the hotels, we saw a whole contingent of American Air Force guys who joined the multitude of other nationalities milling around the bars, restaurants and the beaches. Rumor had it that they brought along their own showers. To be expected, our nightly group ruled. They're Americans, of course they'd bring their showers with them.

***

So Alush was right at the end. Rommel never made it, far from it. At the end he went back to Germany and was assigned to defend the English Channel coast off France from the looming invasions. When the whole thing was over we felt like we had matured a bit, we sort of felt more whole, more knowledgeable about how things worked, and wiser. But no one was really sure of all that.

Viva Victoria

Springfield. There is practically a Springfield in every state of the union. Think about it - it makes sense. The pioneers who founded these places the name came to them naturally, a spring and a field and you've got everything to make a living, start a life, gain sustenance and income. If one equates spring with the seasons, it shows a new beginning, renewed energy and first blooms.

So what better place for the birth of my first granddaughter, coming to see the light of day in Springfield in the middle of spring? There is no better way for a beginning, whether it's in Springfield, MA or Springfield, MO, Springfield is what it is all about, that's what it will say on her birth certificate and in a host of other papers as she makes ready to enter the bureaucratic maze that recognizes one as a person. It will appear in her passport, a document of choice for the adventurous souls.

As you gaze at that beautiful, sweet, delicately perfect little thing, you cannot escape the thoughts coming from the far recesses of one's mind – 'what will she become when she grows up?' A pretentious and unfair question that begs no answer, especially when considering that you are still waiting for this answer yourself.

But the thoughts race on – a ballerina, a famous playwright, a Hollywood goddess, a lawyer, a doctor, and, not to be overlooked is the fact that the time is ripe, certainly around 2030, for a female occupant in the White House. Main thing is that she should be happy. Judging from the happiness she has dispensed so far, she's certainly demonstrated her capability to fully pursue this goal.

You are holding this incredible, little, gorgeous bundle. She is two days old and already projects a personality. It clearly states – "Here is the deal – you people give me comfort and I won't give you trouble. Understood?" She is all demands. She stretches her little body till she gets into a desirable position and then religiously attends to her agenda, set in stone, of eating, burping, passing air, pooping and sleeping. Once in a while of course there is the lung exercise, just testing how loud, how long and how consistently one can holler. She is a day and a night person and the hollering is not confined to any particular part of the twenty four hour cycle. Day runs into night and night runs into day when a little stomach needs to be fed every three hours.

It is amazing to observe how a seven pound little giant exercises control over the lives of people surrounding her. And not just a little control, it is total control. An entire household schedule is radically changed. New equipment galore is being installed. Car seats get tested by the state's authorities. Parents take off from work, which creates a ripple effect on the local economy; or does it? Priorities are realigned. The little person's needs and current presence supersede what was important yesterday. Long term plans are shelved and postponed. The beam of attention is solely aimed at her, whether in her crib, her swing, or sleeping across her mother's or father's chests, definitely the place of choice at this moment. Then there are the events – the baths, diaper changes, the weighing, the check-ups. And she takes it all with aplomb and poise, acknowledging her parents' gratitude when these events pass peacefully, without much yelling and wiggling and wriggling.

After all, little Victoria the 'great' just entered the world. She is trying to establish her niche, push herself into the mayhem of the universe and claim her place. This takes a lot of doing. It is a giant step, very much like landing on the moon and maybe more so. You have to admire her for that. She seems to be doing a good job of it. Then again, she has this terrific support team. An incredible set of parents, committed to little else now and grandparents and a great-grandmother and uncles and aunts and cousins and neighbors and friends. A pretty impressive assembly for one just arrived.

Then come the pictures. What a photogenic subject we have here! The pictures get scanned and beamed to the far corners of the earth within seconds, like AP flashes, and solicit baskets full of kudos in response.

You get to hold her some more. You'd love to do it all day long. What the hell, you are a grandfather and entitled. Others may change diapers. You just hold her, kiss her and photograph her. You only partake in the good stuff. You sling her over your shoulder, she's facing backward. She presses her little head towards yours and her silky ear and cheek meet with your leathery, weathered and aged skin, and it is delicious. A rear view mirror, seeing and enjoying her face would be helpful. Did you hear me Toys-R-Us'?

Or you hold her across your chest and feel the warmth emanating from her little body, the up and down breathing rhythm with deep intervals of sighs and you feel the strength of her legs as they push out and the shape of her back wriggling into place. You get little smacks from her gesticulating arms and when she catches your chin or your finger and grasps it tightly with her strong little hands - it is nothing but short of heaven. And then of course there is the face. Angelic when asleep, expressive when air is passed or rather curious when there is nothing else to do. Who can contain himself not to cover this little face with kisses? It is an unavoidable challenge. So you ask yourself – is there anything better than that around?

Away from her, you lick and smack your tongue with anticipated pleasure as you visualize the great times, the wonderful moments, the incredible joy awaiting you with this little person. Pretty good invention, this being a grandfather. And wait till the grandmother gets into action.

As you walk down the half-deserted streets of Springfield and keep thinking of her – your face gets all screwed up in silly laughter while talking to yourself and describing all the surprises that you will prepare for her and all the surprises that lay in store for you.

The passers-by observe you with concern. Their faces spell out "Who is this nut walking our streets?" "It's OK," I try to reassure them with a half-way intelligent look, "...I do not live here, just passing through."

A Year Later and Very Curious in Missouri

Well, a year went by, Kim the Korean claimed that he has nukes, Saddam lost his throne, a tax cut is in the offing, the economy is still in the basement, there is a surge of love for the French – but so what? Back in Springfield, MO, there is another development that's significant and tangible. Victoria, my granddaughter is establishing her niche in the world and just celebrated her first birthday. Now, that's important.

When one is a bright-eyed, bushy-tailed one year-old and constantly ready for the next adventure, every day and every minute are events of discovery. The little head is cocked, the eyes are shining in anticipation, everything is carefully and thoroughly checked out, be it a face, a whole person, an object or a situation, then a big smile of approval, if it warrants approval of course, is splashed across the little face, spelling in no uncertain terms – OK, let's go, I am ready.

And boy, are we ready. It's like a little sponge, absorbing everything in sight. Unloading a huge supply of curiosity. She needs to know everything, how it works, what it does, and what it sounds like. One cannot discover unless one has an insatiable curiosity. And what is the mark of a curious person? It's sticking your head and your little nose into everything that moves and stands still. Animate and inanimate. It's observing the minutest items with big open eyes and mouth agape in surprise. One studies them thoroughly, chairs, people, faces, crumbs on the floor. And then there are the public areas – the barber shops with mirrors and lights and people stretched in funny positions, shopping malls with lots of traffic, little people making scenes in restaurants, emanating sounds and screams, tempting one to chime in, and one does occasionally by mimicking the other's sounds and creating a stereo effect to accompany the dining pleasure of patrons. And then of course there is Wal-Mart, what a place, lots of friendlies sticking their faces close up and contorting them into smiles. Once in Wal-Mart, the place to be is the hardware department. Why the affinity to the hardware department, you may ask? Well, it's simple, where else do you have an assortment of lighted ceiling fans in perpetual motion? Indeed, an incredible and memorable sight for a little person.

The DISCOVERY CHANNEL does a pretty good job, but in no way can it be compared to this experience of discovery – constantly watching, following and monitoring movements, sticking one's little head way out when a visual obstruction occurs, looking around corners, checking ceilings and trying to swallow the wind when strolling outdoors. Then there is the miracle of things coming off trees, leaves people call them, that only a few months ago crunched in ones hand, yet now, with the advent of spring, the crunch is gone and they are sort of soft and no longer make little noises when trying to crunch them. At every turn, front and center and from the corner of one's eyes, one discovers and discovers. Now that's Discovery.

There are so many fascinating things to see, touch, and taste. Yes, for the ultimate test, it's got to be bitten, possibly chewed - at least it is pleasant on the gums till the teeth show up. Well, let's see, what is one to tackle first? There are the birthday balloons, big things that can be kicked, pushed, and they float. One minute they are out of reach, way, way up on the ceiling, the next minute, at the yank of a string, they come right down and bob on top of one's head. Funny, funny and the colors, all kinds and a little person can handle a whole bunch of them. Then there are the buttons. Grandma's blouse has a whole row of them, and then there are the hats, the funniest thing ever, people look funny in them and they are easy to pull off. Yet when one does, the eyes disappear, faces are covered turning into a peek-a-boo operation that can go on forever.

Traveling by car is much better now, the car seat pointing forward affords one to see the surroundings, check on the traffic and the many colored traffic lights.

Then of course there is grandma and grandpa. The most tolerant people one can meet. They'll talk to you a great deal, feed you with great patience while telling stories and engage one in very interesting facial expressions, very important when one is not yet in command of a vocabulary but speaks the deedle-deedle language no one seems to understand, except of course for grandma and grandpa who can speak it too.

So every day is a curiosity-hunting day. What's this and what's that, discoveries galore, every step of the way. Only the other day one went to have breakfast in grandma and grandpas hotel. So one sat at the table, perched on a high chair - not of the kind at home – but, rather a different looking one. Needs to be checked out. Needs to be gone over thoroughly. The seat belt buckle is different. Shall one test it with one's gums? Indeed an open question until a new discovery replaces this concern. The menus. Look at the size of them, half the size of a little person and the pictures! There are eggs and bread and all sorts of grown-up food in an array of colors. And, lo and behold, one can take the menu and have it sail like a Frisbee over the dining room. One can of course repeat this feat with the scrambled eggs, the bread, and so forth. The problem is the marmalade, it does not fly. So there, a new discovery, marmalade sticks. Not everything can travel the same path or at the same speed. Very interesting. Daddy's face though, is not a very happy face observing this. Daddy does not subscribe to these experiments. They are good for a lab, not in a restaurant.

But it's a treat to go with Daddy into Border's, to go and see where all the books with Elmo, Clifford, and Winnie the Pooh and the whole bunch come from. It's a big store, huge, one cannot see from one end to the other, unless Daddy lets you ride on his shoulders, then one is eight feet off the floor, has a bird's eye view of everything, and I mean everything and one can see and have fun riding Daddy's shoulders while burrowing one's little hands into Daddy's hair or holding on to anything that sticks out, like an ear or two.

Now, this is living. This is fun. Soon one starts to sing and with music comes the dance, the little tush wiggles, the shoulders wriggle, all in tune with the music.

Especially interesting to watch is the other little people. At lunch the other day, the adjacent table sported a family with a whole bunch of kids. They were all over the place, climbing, pushing one another, crawling under the furniture, spilling food and drink – a totally fascinating performance. One was enthralled.

And then there were the inborn social graces. In an assembly of people, Victoria will, with the aplomb of a seasoned cruise director, make sure that everyone is a participant in whatever is transpiring. The little head swivels around in every direction, checking out the faces, lifting an object for viewing, soliciting approval. A campaigner par excellence. No one is neglected, no one is left behind.

Curiosity is practiced in silence, once it is absorbed and downloaded - one opens up and either emulates it, deedle-deedles about it or looks for a repeat confirmation of it. One learns, boy does one learn. There is no profession, no CEO, no General, no President who comes into a job and has to learn so much in a short time. Sitting on a small chair, drinking from a cup, trying to express oneself – it's a task that takes up all the waking hours, all the space between the naps and is done willingly and happily and successfully.

One is in constant readiness, in the Ready-Set-Go mode. Middle names given to people traditionally commemorate relatives and family names, when one name does not fulfill the quota. It's like having two license plates. Friends and peers award nicknames. These usually reflect the character of the person. Thus, I, a proud grandpa, see her as Victoria 'What's-Next' Kaufman.

A year went by and I still walk down the Springfield streets smiling to myself. People still regard me with suspicion, like who is this guy smiling to himself all the time? I try to alley their fears by pointing out that I do not live there, am just visiting. Back at home, friends ask me 'How is Victoria, your granddaughter?' 'How much time you got?' is my answer. I need at least a day to reply.

Three Years later - Frappuccino

It's a dismal Sunday, grey, drizzly as we rode down Campbell Avenue in Springfield, MO. A very lively three year-old held court in the back, identifying every car coming towards us on the other side and triumphantly calling out its make.

Everyone was thinking of a pit stop, and just then a Starbucks came into view.

The three year-old is all gung ho, smacking her little lips in anticipation of something good she was about to choose. We all settled along a settee and she promptly stood up to better observe the place and scan its goings on with an eagle eye.

She observed the system, whereby people would order their coffee and when ready, the barista would call out the designated coffee and they would return to the counter to pick it up. Of course, having been told to behave in a public place, especially in restaurants and not call out as if on a playground, she watched in amazement as the barista kept calling from his perch behind the counter. 'Doesn't he know that this is unacceptable behavior in a restaurant? Very puzzling what these grown-ups allow themselves,' must have gone through her little head.

One call was especially jarring. The barista kept calling "Frappuccino" to no response. At short intervals, he called again and again, and nothing. There is no one there, yet the place is full and thick with people.

After about ten minutes of that, our three year-old straightens up, takes a deep breath and on the top of her silver-bell little voice, she very clearly and resolutely calls out "Frappuccino!" Lo and behold, this time the response is immediate, a bearded guy in a hood jumps up from his dozing, yells "Here, here!" and staggers to the counter to pick up his order to the applause of the entire store.

Had old Schultz of Starbucks been present, I am sure she would have gotten a junior executive job offer. Never underestimate anything, certainly not when it comes to this three year-old.

With all eyes on her, she benevolently smiled at the admiring crowd and calmly went back to ladling out her yogurt.

A Missouri Girl

A Missouri girl is imbued with a high degree of individualism, self-reliance and a strong-willed personality in the best Western pioneering tradition.

Missouri girls' bodies are resilient, flexible and move in tune with any wafting musical sounds, harking back to the covered wagon camp fire fiddler's days of yore. The Missouri girl is an accomplished dancer and singer, eager for fun and music and known to draw all present into the circle of entertainment, with no laggards tolerated.

Rolling laughter, yelps of delight help to locate the Missouri girl. A deep sense of humor and the abstract generates constant mirth and contagious outbreaks.

The Missouri girl has a rare combination of urbanity and ruralism; she is mostly gentle in the salon yet very active in the outdoors. She searches and explores and is enchanted with nature, its flora, fauna and everything that crawls and walks on four legs. She is a hands-on kind of girl with instinctive know-how on how to handle a car, garden utensils, and water hoses and will attack with relish anything with wheels and anything without them, not yet seen before.

The Missouri girl is smart, sharp, and probing until she is completely satisfied that the subject at hand is mastered, her curiosity satisfied and every angle checked before moving on to the next target.

The Missouri girl is voluble. She speaks languages, English and her own. Her expressions are unambiguously clear – No's and Yes's. She is on an acquisition binge, collecting vocabulary, foods, people, and experiences. Once achieved, she is not loathe to celebrate her little victories with a song, a jig and a smile as wide as the entire state. She may engage in lengthy conversations that may suddenly be interrupted with a call of "diaper change!" proclaimed in the manner of a seasoned railroad conductor calling out the stations – and then she is off with a determined I-told-you-so look in her beautiful eyes.

She is a tough chick, yet with a charm that can melt granite. She is an American consumer. She loves food, especially other people's food. She is a social butterfly, yet in a crowd stands her own; she is a snuggler, yet with elbows poised to secure her chosen position.

She is an achiever and she knows it. She looks back on her achievements with benign satisfaction yet embraces every opportunity to climb the next mountain or the next piece of furniture. When in unfamiliar territory, she is a scout checking and making sure the terrain is safe.

Once ascertained that indeed this is so - she is an adventurer, plunging head on into the enticing, yet unknown element to be conquered.

She is athletic, a runner, a climber, a dancer, a champion performer on the park swing and a ball enthusiast. She is also a reader, gobbles up books wholesale, reads and rereads and is at home with the best of them at Barnes & Noble and Border's.

Her interests are wide and reach far afield. She can recite and describe construction equipment and cars and is a regular at the town library analyzing computer programs. She will identify a backhoe from miles away and name the owners of various type cars. She embraces method and discipline, evidenced by her numerically correct counting skills demonstration.

She knows the power of exposure and media. Train a camera on her and she is ready in an instance, looking straight into the lens and yelling "cheeeese."

Thus, this Missouri girl leads a very busy life. Her calendar is full from early morning to bedtime. Event follows event with no time to contemplate. Her stance is in the present and with total concentration of what's around the next corner.

Approaching the fourth anniversary of her being, she is full of anticipation and poised to tackle the coming challenges. Knowing her, these are planned, thought-through and designed to absorb, sponge-like, everything in sight, process it in a business-like manner, clear-eyed and purposeful, then file it in the appropriate departments for opportune use.

So any wonder that I am still strolling the streets of Springfield, laughing, talking, and smiling to myself? One thing is for sure, I'll keep doing it for some time.

Fat Tuesday Coming

The first impression one gets from the Mardi Gras, coming to New Orleans – The Big Easy, is the sense of total integration. Blacks, Whites, Creoles, Cajuns, college students, conventioneers, normal everyday people, transvestites, eccentrics, plain crazies, foreign and domestic tourists, drunks, perverts, cross-dressers, gays, lesbians, locals, white trash, out-of-towners, preppies – all mingle and mix and behave similarly. It's an acceptable and welcoming place.

Why didn't anyone think of this before? The cheapest, most economical and efficient way to integrate the workplace, the schools and society, is for everyone to wear masks. That's it. Mask wearers are the uniform equalizers. Simple and it costs five dollars at the most, OK, with feathers its twelve dollars. Still cheap for what it does.

"You man or woman? Man," I overheard one of the intelligent conversations on the corner of Bourbon and St. Peter, in front of the aptly named Crazy Corner bar and was waiting to witness a Paul Hogan crutch test, attempting to find out whether one faced a woman or a man.

The French Quarter was being renovated. Here and there decrepit houses were subjected to a paint bucket and change their appearance overnight. There is nothing like paint to cover up a multitude of sins, soot and cracks in a wall. The only place though, that has not gotten the preservation treatment is the oddly named and least well-preserved Preservation Hall - the Jazz venue. The hall is the size of two average small living rooms. Half the crowd gets seated on a stepped-up section, while the rest stand in an airless, dinky, dark, musty section, body to pressed body in the best tradition of a New York rush hour subway stuck in a tunnel. The sweet smell of sweat is overwhelming, with new and fresh odors added as the crowds press in closer to make room for more.

But all is forgotten when they start playing, even when the crowd raises its arms and robustly applauds. They have a number of very good seven-man bands. And they play, man, can they play. First they play as an ensemble, then each one does a jam-session type solo and wow, it got better and better and you do not want it to end. Each instrument demonstrates its maximum capability – the cornet, the sax, the clarinet, the trombone, the bases, the piano, and the drums. Each is a tour-de-force and then some. The players are mostly in their fifties and up, seasoned, experienced masters. As I said, the place is a ruin. Come to think of it, maybe they built it and left it that way on purpose. The entrance fee is a modest five dollars and all you can hear.

In honor of Mardi Gras, many of the houses are decorated with the shiny tinsel stuff, papier-mâché masks and naked ladies, both black and white. People saunter up and down the avenues in the most outlandish clothes and, if this does not draw enough attention, there is always mooning, or taking off your top, flipping tits wildly to the cheering and the delirious college kids, hanging from the balconies and the rafters and throwing down anything that comes to hand, sometimes even themselves in a drunken stupor.

Bourbon Street is dangerous to pass. It was the Times Square of New Orleans before they cleaned it up. I had something land on me when behind me a woman took off her top. I believe it was a ball, it came down from the second floor and bounced off my head. It was aimed at her, a bad aim and I got the full brunt.

The whole Mardi Gras business is overhyped, overrated and over-priced. But it is a hell of a business proposition. No way could they fill up all the hotels, draw conventions to the city, if not for the aura the city fathers lend to the name.

Corruption is a tradition in New Orleans and Louisiana. Standing at one of the parade routes, a stretched limo with suits in it waved to the public lining the route. I asked a black woman, who enthusiastically cheered the floats but took a breather when the limo passed, if it was the mayor in there? "If it's not him, then it's another crook," she yelled over the din.

She may have had a point. After all, former governor Edwards was finally indicted after twenty years of investigations and trials and may spend some time in jail. Edwards was a bon vivant and knew how to spend the public purse on foreign trips – all for the good of New Orleans, of course. If he had had more than two arms, he would have been accompanied by more than two ladies. I met him in Paris, at Spie-Batignolles, the French engineering company I was consulting. He was going to use the firm for oil exploration in Louisiana. He came in on a private jet and behaved like royalty. Everything went, everything that was not nailed down. He drawled his way, using his Louisiana French and charmed the pants off everybody. Then he took their money and left via the Riviera. He would repeat these junkets as often as a few times a year. I am sure he will have white tablecloth with silver service while in jail.

The French Quarter is laid out in a grid, very convenient and com-fortable. Towards the river, the mighty Mississippi, is Jackson Square. It's framed on one end with the St. Louis Cathedral and symmetrically positioned to either side of it, the two French style buildings housing Louisiana State Museum historical exhibits, including in one of them, one of the three existing death masks of Napoleon and in the other, the

Carnival Museum, everything you want to know and do not want to know about Mardi Gras.

Mardi Gras is a year-round industry and yes, people make a good living of it, it seems. The floats are built year round, too. To me they all look the same, just painted differently. What a racket. Bead chains are big and everyone is wearing a collection that grows by the hour and day around every available neck. Larger ones are in fashion, for the mostly larger people one sees. Of course, all the millions of beads worn, bought and traditionally tossed from the floats are all made in China, where else?

People are big all right. Six feet plus and three to four hundred pound mid-westerners, with the ladies in shorts and legs reminiscent of the California Redwoods. Once they stopped growing in height, it seems, they started growing in width without missing a beat. I guess when you are in the middle of the Prairie, one looks puny, no matter the size and weight. But wait till you enter a small door. It is especially noticeable when a group or an individual comes into a crowded restaurant and is sitting at one of the dainty French tables. It becomes apparent that America is definitely overweight. The saying about the wife looking like a truck is not a joke here. It is close to reality, and some are certainly the size of an SUV.

Yet, none of this prevents anyone of these giants from standing in line for hours at Café Du Monde – the best place in town for Beignets. They are really good. Actually they are simple donuts, but better, more delicate and done differently. Du Monde specializes in coffee and beignets and that's it. And they do it twenty-four hours a day. They never close. To avoid the lines, one has to get up at seven and rush over before the onslaught starts. They are extremely well organized, and as soon as one grabs a table, the waiters appear. The Beignets are superb and fresh, and hot coffee and juice appear soon afterwards. All the waiters seem to be Vietnamese. They smile, are friendly, very efficient, and seem to be puzzled by what all the fuss is about.

You can traipse along the mighty Mississippi to Jackson Square and beyond, along the promenade called the Moon Walk, named after the Jimmy Walker of New Orleans, Mayor Landrieu Moon, who was mayor forever, got rich in the process, was a powerful politician and left his Moon tracks all over New Orleans.

Acme was another gold mine of a food place. They served local food and managed to have lines in front of their store from early morning to late at night. Once inside, it is organized mayhem. Yelling, screaming, and small and large tables filled with people. Beer comes in buckets and heaping plates of crayfish and crawfish and bratwurst are handed around. Prices are reasonable, accounting for the lines outside. At tables with six or more, there was always a moron who was the joker of the group. This added thousands of decibels to the already ear-splitting din. This joker says something, and immediately it is followed by giant outbursts of choking laughter cascading endlessly around the table and competing with adjacent tables that sport their own jokers. It is very much like hearing an artillery shell leave a muzzle, fly overhead and culminate in a huge explosion. You'd try to get a bite down before it 'hit,' an endless, repeating process. When leaving Acme into the noisy streets, your ears come back to normal, enjoying the sounds of the street, so benign in comparison to Acme.

Cemeteries are the big thing. The graves of the Queen of Voodoo and all sorts of other such creatures are shrines for pilgrims. Cemetery tours are heavily advertised and no horse and buggy ride would be complete without at least one cemetery. Some of the mausoleums are big enough to open a McDonald's and I am sure it would do a land office business there. One gets hungry touring graves.

What we missed seeing is a funeral, except for the Jazz Funeral Bar. Funeral processions offer the best Jazz show in town. I guess no one dies during Mardi Gras.

The Natchez is a paddle wheeler. It's a large ship or boat or river steamer. It is powered by steam, which turns the fire-red painted paddle wheel in the rear of the ship, and makes a lot of noise blowing its whistle as it slides up and down the Mississippi with a Jazz band playing on board. The trip takes about two hours. It is not very scenic except that being on the water is pleasant and the cruise is very comfortable.

The French Market is of course in the French Quarter, or actually at its edge, right after the gilded statue of Joan of Arc. The Market has two parts, food and clothing – meaning T-shirts, hats and other tourist paraphernalia. The food part is interesting, with lots of Tabasco and other related products. Avery Island, off New Orleans and the McIhlenny family have been makers of Tabasco since shortly after the Civil War. When McIhlenny came back from the war, he found an abandoned French perfume factory on Avery Island, his home. Since they were growing peppers on the island and he had an old recipe for pepper sauce from Tabasco, Mexico, he decided to get into the pepper sauce business. There was scarcity of materials and goods after the war in the South, but that did not deter McIhlenny; he found a large supply of bottles in the abandoned perfume factory destined for perfume bottling. McIhlenny named his product Tabasco and bottled it in the French perfume bottles, as it is still done today. Hence the distinct shape of the Tabasco bottles.

New Orleans runs the oldest streetcar in the world. This distinction also goes to Calcutta in India. You board at Canal and Condelette, make an almost U-turn into St. Charles, go by the Le Circle, which is round even in French, and then go through the Garden District, where the rich people live and straight on to Tulane and Loyola Universities, all the way to Carrolton where you get off and on again for the return trip. Once in a while an automobile stalls as it tries to cross the tracks, the streetcar stops, the conductor invites the able-bodied to come down and push and then the streetcar keeps going on its appointed rounds. The windows are open, the wooden benches are comfortable and it is a good way for sightseeing the city. Tulane and Loyola are tightly packed next to each other, with lots of parkland all around.

There are a few Stanley Kowalski types walking around carrying mini-buckets of beer that are a good match to the passing Streetcar

Named Desire. There is also a Drive and a Parkway in another part of town named Desire. Just picture Tennessee Williams, walking down Royal or Chartres Avenue, next to the St. Louis Cathedral in a small alley. Adjacent to the corner bar and restaurant is the house where William Faulkner wrote his first play, "A Soldier's Pay." The street section of the yellow painted house features the William Faulkner Bookstore. A few more steps down another alley, off Chartres, is the house where Degas painted while in New Orleans. And across the street, a bit towards Esplanade, on Bourbon, is the former blacksmith shop of Jean Lafitte, the famous French pirate leader, who settled in New Orleans after receiving a pardon for helping the United States in the 1812 war against the British. Now, that's a good pardon, as pardons go nowadays. Today, the blacksmith shop is, what else, a twenty-four hour bar.

Coming in and leaving from the airport, one passes the Superdome, an ugly covered concrete monster. It looks pretty new. Back in the city, people were walking around, mostly in a daze with these huge plastic cups, actually mini-buckets filled with beer. Signs all over offered "Take Out Beer $1.00." How can one refuse a bargain like that? At a poetically named bar on Bourbon called The Stream Pit, there is a large sign that reads: "Huge Ass Beers to Go." Now this really is an offer no one can refuse and no one does.

The more sophisticated drunks can avail themselves of a sixteen ounce Bloody Mary Take-Out for $4.00; the zombies walk the street with both hands holding cups. If they should ever lose their pants, they wouldn't have a free hand to catch them. They walk and puke, drink some more and puke some more.

Once in a while, to demonstrate a semblance of authority and law, one sees plainclothes cops walking down the street to the Royal Street's 8th Police Precinct, leading a handcuffed and mostly heavily tattooed person. I say person, not due to my PC consciousness, but rather that it is hard to make out the gender of the one being led away. Some of the handcuffees look morose, others are floating in space and still others are engaged in lively chats with their captors. The Police Station is housed in a former ornate bank building. As one enters, there is a white, carved sergeant's desk. Behind, hang three crystal chandeliers. In front is a little garden with chairs and tables, café style.

The police share power with the Sheriff's office. It is a very powerful office in the Louisiana parishes, as the counties are called here. The Sheriff commands an army of deputies who constantly vie for turf with the police. They are two distinct power blocks, not necessarily working with each other. The Chief is a black former cop, the Sheriff, a three-hundred-pound-white, cigar chomping Southerner, with a stained Panama hat and who likes to go fishing. In the press, the Chief and the Sheriff attack each other, but in private they go fishing together. I've got to go and find the black lady who pointed out the crooks to me and see what she has to say about these guys.

Canal Street is the main venue for parades. These originate in various parts of town and mostly pass Canal Street where they swing into St. Charles, thus passing the French Quarter and continuing to Uptown, Maitiere and other parts. Dominating Canal Street is the Rubinstein Bros. Men and Ladies Clothes sign. It is lit, it rotates and mingles constantly with the big colorful floats. This is called strategic advertising. Are there Jewish Cajuns?

The custom is for the float attendants to fling bead strings at the crowd and for the crowd to catch them. This results in outstretched arms and hands every time a float passes by. Screaming accompanies this, very much like at a football game or other stadium competitions. The crowds materialize from nowhere and stand along the routes awaiting the parades. To local entrepreneurs this affords a captive audience opportunity for selling things. All one needs is a supermarket cart or a home shopping cart, load it up and start selling. Offerings range from teddy bears to stuffed little alligators, beads, masks and other interesting stuff. Condoms are hawked at big discount prices. Marijuana too, is sold, adroitly placed under the condom pack in one swift swooping transaction. All this goes on while thousands stand around, the bands blare, hundreds of cops straddle the street corners and in the distance there are groups of mounted police chatting with one another and everyone is happy.

I figured that beer must flow like a river. Indeed, large Budweiser trucks roam the little narrow streets of the Quarter day and night. I wondered why no one had laid a pipeline yet, it would alleviate motor traffic.

The streets are trashed every few hours. In the mornings, it looks like fall in the east when leaves are piled high, only here it is garbage. The sanitation workers come armed with huge shovels and shovel all morning till they get down to the original asphalt street covering. As soon as they are gone, stuff starts flying again.

Royal Street is a rather interesting street when one takes the time to look a bit closer at the stores along it. It is a section of antique stores and art galleries. The antiques are of high quality, not the pedestrian junk one usually encounters. It is of a Christie, Sotheby, and Doyle level with very interesting and rare pieces. Some of the galleries feature good art and are worth a visit.

At certain hours of the day, Royal Street is closed to traffic. As soon as the barriers go up, groups of musicians and street performers install themselves along the middle of the street. There are good Cajun bands, mountain folks from who knows where and, of course, lots of Jazz and sundry other groups – all blowing and strumming away, some rather well. It is a portrait of the Sixties, reenacted by a new generation. No one misses a beat.

On Royal Street too is the famous Brennan. It serves a thirty-five and a forty-five dollar breakfast. I remember from the time they had a branch restaurant next to the skating rink in Rockefeller Center in New York. Brennan's fame evolved from the times when New Orleans society was carousing and celebrating the nights away, with gambling, brothels, card playing and other important pursuits. At dawn, when the worn out crowds returned to their homes and beds, they came into Brennan's who served a hearty dinner-breakfast, so the revelers could rest on a full stomach. The menu was tremendous, which was a problem. We could not eat it, not even a smidgen of it, what with the champagne and strawberries and steaks and fish and eggs and sausages and shrimp from the Gulf and hams and bacon and beignets and a whole list of things I never heard of. All topped by sumptuous desserts and cigars and cognac. One needed to train for that, or be a lot younger, as I was when I had had it years ago. Brennan is situated in a pink multistory building with jazz bands assisting in the digestion.

Further down towards Canal is the Court of Two Sisters with a through-the-block outlet to Bourbon Street. A permanent Jazz band is the attraction for diners. Music is all over the place. In front of the Cathedral there are a number of bands playing. In front of Jackson Square there are bands and street performers. This in addition to individual players and performers on every street corner.

Coming off the Natchez upon returning to port, a rapper was serenading the ganglplank. I recall a line that caught my attention:

"…remember, be happy, I sit here sing and carouse, or I be out there, robbing your house." Makes sense to me. There are a lot of pantomimists - people standing as statues all over the place. Sometimes it was hard to notice the real from the fake, unless one watched the pigeons, they do not get fooled, they bombard the real statues, but will not spend one dropping on the breathing ones.

The streets all have French names. The former Spanish influence is maintained in beautiful, white and blue tiles inset into the wall on the street corner, recalling the names in Spanish. Royal Street, would be Calle Real, or St. Ann Street is Calle Santa Ana. The juxtaposition of the Spanish, the French, the British, the American, the Creole, the Cajun and the African is very much apparent. On top of all that there is a generous dollop of Voodoo. And not to forget the Jews and German farmers who were brought there to settle and farm the area. It is a Jambalaya in the true sense, comparable to the melting-pot description of what makes up New York.

Next to the French Market is a lovely little courtyard and a building that belongs to the city or state. There are free Jazz performances there by known groups, very much like at the Preservation Hall. Across the street there are a number of cafes and, on the opposite side, is a long arcade promenade. Each has groups of musicians playing. So, when strolling around the quarter, one is never without music. Then there are the one-tune players. Fellows equipped with a trumpet or trombone, which play one and the same tune over and over again. They certainly have stamina, something that cannot be said for the listeners.

One cannot mention New Orleans without mentioning the super-star, the master of all, the one and only "Satchmo" Louis Armstrong. At the edge of the Quarter, on Rampart, is a park named Armstrong Park. In the park is a statue of Louis Armstrong holding his trumpet in one hand and his famous handkerchief in the other.

One cannot leave the Quarter without making the rounds in a horse drawn buggy. The clipity-clap of the horse adds to the ambiance. One travels through it and makes room for the other buggies to pass by the narrow street. It is very enjoyable. All the drivers or coachmen are performers. Man or woman, they are characters and act out their parts. They dispense pearls of wisdom and some information that should be double-checked later. I overheard one profound piece of wisdom from another cab "…it ain't the mules that's stubborn – people is." I did not know this.

Off we go to the swamps to see mosquitoes, alligators and the occa-sional Cajun. We want to see how the Cajuns live. Actually we should have driven down to Houma and along the Gulf, that's where the heart of the real stuff is, but this required a few more days that we did not have. I actually plotted out a route going up to Baton Rouge, west to Lafayette, turn southeast to Houma and back to New Orleans. As a short-cut we went to the swamps which were about twenty miles west of New Orleans. A nice little bus picked us up and got us to the landing at the swamp where we found a flat, comfortable raft-like boat. One can also take an airboat; that is the contraption with an airplane propeller in the back that makes it skim over the water and over land. We skipped that for a more leisurely two-hour trip into the bayous and waterways.

While waiting for the raft's departure, we look around the Cajun surroundings. Some houses were villa types, made of brick and on tended and landscaped plots. Cadillacs are parked in the driveways. What is the main bone of contention in a Cajun divorce? asks an old joke. Answer: Who gets the trailer? Indeed, there are many trailers strewn around the area. The people all seem busy with fishing, tourism and riding their motorcycles. No rider is qualified, it seems, unless covered with tattoos from head to toe. So you stand there and see a lot of artwork pass by at accelerating speeds.

One of the villas probably owned by the boat operators features a basketball court next to the waiting area with two regulation balls available for the customers to entertain themselves until the boat departs. It is a rather unique and very efficient idea. No one complains if the departure is late.

Alligators swam around the raft. It was very nice, I liked the landscape. The captain was a Cajun, dressed in camouflage fatigues and Nike sneakers with a long knife on his belt. He must have developed a sense of humor over the years answering the questions of the tourists he ferried. People wanted to see a full-grown alligator. We came to a turn, like a cul-de-sac waterway and he alerted us that a big alligator, "…just as you wished" happened to be sitting, sunning himself at the edge. Since alligators can sit in a motionless, pantomime position, very much like the street artists in New Orleans, I was not sure whether this was a stuffed one or real and there were no pigeons in sight for testing. So we all assumed he was real. And maybe he or she was.

The first night in New Orleans we had dined at the Bayona, a white table-cloth place, with nicely served food, tranquil surroundings, tastefully appointed. Antoine is another place with a good reputation and there are many others. I wonder what this place is like without a Mardi Gras. I am told by my friend Ed, who was there on an ophthalmology convention during Halloween, that it was almost like a Mardi Gras. It's understandable. The Big Easy is set up for partying. It is a partying city. It is easy to do here.

On the last night we had dined at Sabrina+Gabriel, not bad, not good, certainly overrated, but they had space and that meant something. The night before we could not get in anywhere, so we went to Walgreens. They have a refrigerator where they offer packed sandwiches. That night we dined Walgreen-style.

Our hotel was situated on Royal Street, two buildings from Canal, in the heart of the French Quarter. This proved to be very convenient and comfortable – one stepped out on the street and was right in the middle of it all. We had a view on Canal Street and could tell when the parades were showing up.

The Walgreens on the corner of Royal Street and Iberville Street is housed in a former bank building. That bank issued the first ten-franc coin denominations, called Dix. When the Americans took over, the pronunciation changed and evolved into the general description of the South as Dixie.

Bujana

Bujana is a competent, middle-aged lady, recently from Poland, strong of build and effervescent of temper, eager to understand and to please in her daily work of cleaning apartments in New York City. A pleasant, willing sort.

Her command of the English language is admittedly rather narrow, but she believes that it is less than it actually is. In her eagerness to accommodate, she'll agree to almost anything that is said and then proceed with polishing the wrong end of the stick. Her lack of English language confidence is even more pronounced on the phone.

Bujana shares an apartment with her cousin, Tadeusc, who has already been in America for over ten years. They live in a neighborhood adjacent to Greenpoint, the Polish stronghold in Brooklyn. Tadeusc is a man of dignity and in his late fifties or early sixties, an avid reader of Polish newspapers and someone who constantly complains about the lack of formality and politeness in New York. His experiences of New York life seem to richly provide him with endless subjects, ample case histories, and numerous personal encounters and examples; he happily and endlessly dwells on it. Intermittently he cocks his head, shakes it horizontally in total disapproval and launches into the art and quality of Polish civilization, culture, customs and habits.

***

Tadeusc's command of English is not much better than Bujana's. It seems at times that it might even be less so. Bujana has a greater imagination and what she does not understand she sometimes puts together by observing body and facial motions, adding a dollop of guesswork and voila, she pronounces the result. Tadeusc on the other hand is a methodical, systematic, robot-like thinker unburdened by any spark of humor and he surely would never engage in the undignified sport of guessing. However Bujana convinced herself that Tadeusc is in total command of English and is imbued with a deep understanding of all things and any works in English. So when called on the phone by an English speaker, before the first "Hi" is exchanged, the cry goes out, "Tadeusc!" whereupon he promptly appears on the phone with his trademark, solemn response: "Problem?"

***

I am lucky to have Bujana take care of the cleaning chores in my apartment. She has the keys and a free run of it at her convenience. Since I am never there when she comes by, and months pass without us seeing or talking to each other, when the need arises I contact her by phone in the evening. A recent encounter put my resources of describing a tree to the test, and all for naught.

Me: "Hi, Bujana, how...."

Bujana: "Tadeusc, Tadeusc...!"

Tadeusc: "Problem?" Tadeusc, true to form, announces solemnly.

Me: "Hi Tadeusc – no problem, give me back Bujana."

Me: "Bujana!"

Bujana: "Yes, yes…no Tadeusc?"

Me: "No, no, You…."

Bujana: "Ok, Ok, I come Th-e-resdaytoosday." Bujana always fused the two days into one. Indeed, with their similar sounds, they may sound the same to non-English speakers. To make sure, Bujana always nailed both of them down.

Me: "No Bujana, this is not why I am calling you. Listen," I then proceed into adagio mode, "…listen please, the tree that stands next to the window, the green thing, please water it every time you come, okay?"

Bujana: "Yes, yes, I make window very good."

Me: "Not the window, Bujana, the tree, the plant, the thing with the green leaves on it."

Bujana: "Tadeusc, ahh, Tadeusc," Bujana murmurs in exasperation trying to hold on to something that is not there.

Tadeusc: "Problem?" Tadeusc reappears with his stoic, self important voice.

Me: "Tadeusc, please tell Bujana to put water into the tree that stands in the golden metal pot."

Tadeusc: "Water? Ohhhh big problem, no pots?"

Me: "No, no, no, tell her to water it, with a can."

Tadeusc: "Water where? Oh oh oh…what to do? Water big problem."

Me: "The tree, the plant, the bush."

To this, Tadeusc wakes up, the political implications seem interesting and for the first time he believes he seems to grasp what this is all about.

Tadeusc: "B---u-sh?" he exclaims in a heavily accented and intoned Polish.

Me: "No, no Tadeusc, give me Bujana, not Bush, forget Bush."

Tadeusc: "Oh, you Democrat?"

Me: "Bujana! Bujana!"

Bujana: "Yes, yes…okay window, water, okay, Th—eresdaytoosday, two o'clock, okay?"

Me: "Thank you Bujana, thank you."

In total mental and physical exhaustion I drop the phone, collapse on the couch and fall into a deep fitful sleep. The solution came through a dear old friend of mine, a former Polish cavalry officer who lives in a distant state. I wrote a series of pertinent messages projecting into the future; he translated them into Polish and emailed them to me. Watering the plant was one of them. I then enlarged the slogans, pasted them on eight and a half by eleven colored boards and positioned them all over the apartment at strategic locations Bujana couldn't miss. Bless her.

Madison

My name is Madison Kaufman and I am a dog. I come from a non-denominational family, must have had a slew of siblings; but who remembers?

I landed in Springfield on top of a hill, with a next door neighbor Lilly, who is seldom seen, but when she is, she's a great friend.

I was very small when I landed there, I really love them all a lot, lots of people there. Especially the little girl Vicki – she's not so little now, but then she was. She's like my sister, sometimes like a mother and she teaches me things. She loves me to the sky and carries me around a lot of times whether I want to or not. But what is a dog to do? I love the whole family - the Mom really loves me and all the others, they love me a lot, too. I was really lucky. Sometimes I think about it, like when I snooze, which I do a lot, then I wake up happy and look around to do something.

The Dad and the Mom are all so cuddly, I love to lie across their chests or their tummies, really comfy and I appreciate it a lot. And when they sleep and I really, really want to relax, I make myself comfortable on top of their heads. The big guy, though, makes little noises through his nose, sometimes not so little, but I don't move from there once I make myself comfortable. No matter, the snoring. Then there is the uncle, of course, who calls himself Mike. I go on car trips with him sometimes, and he really takes care of me. We walk a lot together and I wish he could talk my language so we could have a conversation. Then there are the old folks who come once in a while from another place altogether. They all love me, too, and the old guy is always trying to start a conversation, talks to me till my head hurts and I remember him doing it on the Skype too, woofing and talking and thinking I understand his chatter. By the way, I am on Skype, with my picture. The lady called grandma loves me, too, and I love it when they rub my tummy, oh, I could have it last all day.

A dog's life is not an easy one, what with resting, sleeping, eating and jumping up and down, walking the park and - get this - going sometimes, maybe on my birthday again, to the dog run. Now this is something more than a little dog like me can bear. I go bananas, I love it so much.

But the best is when the big guy is operating in the kitchen. Oh does he cook delicious stuff! And he used to let me taste it, but no more. I have had problems with my stomach, so now I can only eat special foods the doctor prescribed, otherwise I'll have to walk around with that stupid diaper. Oh doggone do I hate that. What will other dogs think when they see that? But for that food I am really sad, the food was so good, and now I do not have this to look forward to anymore. That's real sad, and, for me, it is a big quality of life issue. I mean, come on, you want to enjoy yourself a little bit once in a while and when the smells from the kitchen hit me, I am ready to pounce, and I would , had I been bigger. I just love that kitchen.

Sometimes I go to the groomer, and to tell you the truth, I am glad when I am out of there. It is not pleasant at all, all that picking and poking and stupid talk from the lady shampooist. Sometimes I look good and sometimes, if indeed it is me I see in the mirror, I think I see a plucked chicken.

What people don't know is that I am an expert on their toes and shoes. I got a front seat and look at them all the time from a level they never see. And you know what else I like? When I am not tired? To go outside and chase those dumb squirrels - do they get scared when I chase them, they just come and sit in my yard like it belongs to them, and I've got to show them once in a while who is boss.

Well, to be honest, it's a lot of work to look relaxed, calm, well-behaved and happy. Actually, come to think of it – I am. I've got a good life, good family, good people, good entertainment, lots of kissing and belly rubbing and stroking. On a bad hair day I don't mind, who cares which direction my hair goes? But on a good hair day, it gets too much sometimes. And I love my sister and friend and protector, oh my how I love her, but I got to be careful since I am not as young anymore as I used to be. The other day I couldn't wait to get down the stairs fast enough and we all thought I broke a leg. That was real stupid.

I'll tell you a secret though, I like to do stupid things, and they are the best. Let the people waddling around me do the smart things, I'll stick to the stupid stuff. And I'd also like to stick to the good food the big guy is making in the kitchen, Oh my, when can I have that again? It's really what I am thinking about all the time.

I got to go rest now, because when the old guy comes to town soon, he'll start talking to me, asking me questions and looking into my eyes. And he always starts with "Wooof, Wooof!" and thinks he speaks my language doing it. Speak English for God's sake I try to tell him. So I want to make sure I don't fall asleep on him. But I like him and he loves me. I also like to see him dance the way I do when I get excited and he sticks his tongue out the way I do, exactly. How does he do that? Maybe it's something only old people can do, but he won't tell you.

Savannah

It's all geared up for tomorrow. ETA: Seven o'clock in the morning. Our ship was coming in. Not the kind that would alleviate all one's worries and deposit a huge pile of money. No, it was a real ship. The Zim Savannah, a brand new ship, barely out of the yard, carrying new eight by eight by forty foot shipping containers, made of silvery, bright aluminum like no other container. All and everything was redesigned for the brand new division of this shipping company that had hired my services as an image and marketing consultant.

Butterflies abounded in anticipation of the following day, but every one of the group of technical consultants and company executives milled around in the bar acting like they didn't have a care in the world. What a bunch of liars - first they drank to excess trying to relax each other and then, in tandem, smoked nervously to excess, creating this thick smoke screen, so they could perhaps disappear behind it. Repeated sudden runs to the phones, arguments that increased beyond normal decibel range, and unwarranted cheerfulness revealed the little flutterings going on deep in their stomachs.

Well, tomorrow morning we shall see it all. The media was mobilized, helicopters would be hovering galore, local and national television would be present, as well as all the editors of the local print media. The hope was for the weather to hold up. Savannah was supposed to be calm with only some drizzle but, at Fort Sumter, a short distance down the coast, the winds were picking up.

'Our ship is coming around the bend there, but what's a little wind when sailing the high seas?' I mulled. 'And this time, the cannons will be silent.'

For me, it was the culmination of a lengthy effort to finally see this maiden voyage and the inauguration of the port materialize. Everything was new and this, to use a marine term, was really the shakedown event, to make sure and seal the fact that everything worked as planned. Every element of this was brand new. The operating company, its ship, and its port were all equipped with advanced, computerized technology.

The ship slated to arrive made its way through the Panama Canal, coming from Japan and Hong Kong on its maiden voyage. It was a big deal. This event inaugurated the port of Savannah as a container port, a distribution hub to all points in the South and a base for the Far East trade.

The confluence of all these "firsts" woke up this lovely town and it could not have happened to a better place. With marketing in mind, I was constantly on the lookout for opportunities to trumpet the event. The governor was coming over from Atlanta with his retinue of department heads to witness the opening of the port, with all its new and fancy moving gantries, characteristic of the container ballet at a modern port, going from the ship to the trucks and back again.

It was a big day for Savannah and for the governor, who pushed for business development in these parts. Before now, Far East trade with the South had to unload in New Jersey and then be trucked down to the South. Now, delivery would be direct. For us, on behalf of the ship line and its new base, it was a triple header of inaugural events like few others before: the ship, the port, the new trade route.

Still in the bar, people tried to keep their excitement subdued - at least I did and tried to get some sleep in the hours that were left. People filed out slowly, trying to call it a night. Plans were hatched to be up by five and orders were filed with the kitchen to assure an early breakfast.

"Make sure you wake me on time!" the call went out.

Little did we know that we would be woken up, only not at the time we had designated.

***

Vintage WWII vessels carrying bulk cargo had been the heart of the company, which had been operating in the Far East and hauling goods for the early importers in the New York - New Jersey area at the lowest rates in the trade. That was also the reason they were often forgiven for tardy arrivals and deliveries.

Then one day, the decision had been made to convert to all container ships. State-of-the-art vessels were ordered in rapid succession, new containers were designed, a new division was spun off under separate management, and the entire operation - ships, ports, trucking, shipping, logistical support, and marketing was computerized with the aid of the most advanced technology available at the time.

Eager "Young Turks" were installed to run it, all of them know-it-alls, MIT and Technion-Haifa graduates holding either degrees in engineering or operational research PhD's. Investing hundreds of millions of dollars, the division became an autonomously operated unit of the company - and a good thing it did. It was not only the right move, it was a necessary step if one wanted to stay relevant. It probably also prevented murder within the firm. The parent company, headed by an old timer, who admittedly lived in the past and had a strict entitlement mindset, operated with a management style directly opposite that of the "Young Turks." There was no chance that these two approaches would be reconciled, so the expansion kept that issue off the table.

I gladly accepted when invited by the "Young Turks" to assist their new division in creating an image for their impeccable, cutting-edge service that would divorce it from the old bulk carrier image and its business reputation. In tandem, I was to expand this into a bang-up marketing campaign, with advertising and public relations. I liked their gung-ho attitude and deemed it an interesting project to get involved with.

The selling points were the most clear-cut I have ever seen: state of the art ships with superior designs, bar-coded containers, and a comput-er-controlled system locating containers at an instant, as well as comput-erizing port operations. All designed by a crop of top experts from world-renowned schools.

The ships indeed looked beautiful: clean-cut, well-shaped, with sky-scrapers of container boxes piled up high on their decks and in their specially designed holds. All one could say about the containers - the endless rows of shiny, silver, sparkling metal boxes gleaming in the sun - was that they were an impressive sight. The containers were made in Pennsylvania by Strick, and were sold by the thousands by a super salesman.

A bit belatedly, the weight issue came into play. It must have hap-pened during the decal application time, when the box was being weighed. The more the box weighs the less cargo it can hold, less cargo, less revenue income for the company. The new shiny box seemed to be overweight. The last I heard about the problem was, "We are working on it." I also heard the old joke - "What's heavier, a ton of goose feathers or a ton of steel?" Eventually, of course, the problem was resolved. Containers are the core of the intermodal shipping method. Their size and weight is critical in terms of fitting on trucks, trains, barges, and planes. When traveling over the roads, too, they must abide by weight restrictions. Weigh stations, located along highways, monitor weight limits and try to keep everyone honest.

The only other question was how to exploit the shift to container ships such that containers wouldn't have to be unloaded in New Jersey and brought all the way South. I thus spoke with the young engineers driving the company's reorganization and gave them some advice.

The company's shipping routes originated at Far Eastern ports, then sailed the Panama Canal and went north to Port Elizabeth in New Jersey to discharge their cargo, sailing around the southern United States. Instead of bypassing the South and then having extra shipping routes from New Jersey to the southern US, it would make much more sense, it seemed to me, to drop off goods destined for the South on the way to New Jersey, thus accomplishing everything in one run.

"You guys should stop off somewhere in the South along the coast," I said.

"Good idea. Do you have a place in mind?" the Young Turks challenged me in unison, trying to hide their sarcastic smiles.

"No, not yet. But I think you should work on it."

"How? Are you going to work it out? With whom?" the most out-spoken of them asked, with a sly smile.

"With whom? Simple. With you!" I shot back, for lack of a better answer.

Work it out we did. We pored over the map, went up and down the East Coast and kept looking. The more I looked, the more I wanted to vacation there, it sounded so nice. Fort Sumter was there, and here was Savannah. I could picture the moss-covered trees in front of the southern mansions and I suspected the food must be good, too.

"Hold on for a moment," the big PhD boss said, "…we need a port with facilities, with gantries, the whole shebang, and which port will have that? In Elizabeth, we have that and it's a huge investment if you don't. They have ports like Elizabeth?"

"I am looking at a positive bottom line, of course. Yes, there will be an investment, but your business will die if you do not introduce new and better ways to handle it. Your containers rolling from just Elizabeth will be road kill for your competition. Think of that."

***

The more I kept thinking about it, the more I liked Savannah. The fastest way to get this going would be to go to the governor. We offered an international shipping line that was able, ready, and willing to open a loading and unloading facility right there in sleepy Savannah, turn it into a state-of-the art container port, bring jobs, and add to the city's business hub. The company would invest, but wanted the state to contribute its share and, first of all, build adequate roads to make the harbor accessible to trucks. Sounded good. So how did one get to the governor? I decided to try calling.

My phone call to the governor's office was accepted and I was invited to come down and meet with Governor Jimmy Carter. If we could manage to come the following Tuesday, he had an all-day with his business development team, who would be eager to lend an ear.

Joining me in this adventure was Hy Tabak, an eminent intermodal business expert and the author of textbooks about it, Gideon, the shipping company executive, and another fellow named Alex, who was a sort of quiet type and didn't talk much at meetings. In the past, however, he had made it known what he thought of eighty percent of his colleagues, and was a whiz with putting the plant engineering together for a container port structure. As icing on the cake, I brought along my old buddy Al Kaplan, an advertising maven. A tail gunner during the war, he had gained his own perspective from this vantage point and, consciously or not, adapted it to the endeavors of his trade.

***

The Georgia governor's office was located on the street level of the State Capitol. As we entered the lobby and tried to find our bearings, a balding gentleman in a dark, tie-less suit rolled up to me on a sort of huge tricycle. Before I had a chance to ask for directions, he called out to me from a distance:

"Who you people looking for?"

"Oh, thank you, we're looking for the Governor's office. Is it to the right or…."

Without letting me finish my sentence, he responded, "What d'you want with him? I'm the Lieutenant Governor," he proclaimed, straightening out on his tricycle. "See," pointing to his contraption, "…this gets me around quick here. You can tell me."

"That's very smart, sir," I said, admiring his tricycle.

"You can talk to me," he said.

"We have a meeting scheduled with the governor. Which way is it? Left or right?" I now firmly stated.

"You can talk to me. I'm the Lieutenant Governor," he repeated somewhat impatiently.

"I know, you told me."

"What's it about?"

"Important stuff."

With that, we marched away. Concerns set in. 'What's the governor like if this is his Lieutenant? Perish the thought. Let's go and see.'

Finally, we found the place. As we were ushered into the Governor's office, he came to the door to greet us. There were people already in the room. After exchanging pleasantries and having a short photo-op session by the official State photographer, it was down to business. The Governor, his experts arrayed behind him, was knowledgeable, business-like, and exuded efficiency. He was an extremely friendly guy with an easy laugh. Before I even had a chance to say some introductory words and play our spiel of how we chose Savannah as part of our business model and how we intended to develop the port further and make it a permanent home base on our Far East route, the Governor thanked us for coming and was very grateful for our choosing Savannah, a place for which he'd always had a soft spot in his heart, from the days when he was a kid visiting with his parents. He would extend all the assistance he could, as part of furthering his economic development agenda for the state in general and for Savannah in particular.

"It is not every day that a confluence of interests, opportunity, and geographical location meet at precisely the right time and place," I told him. "Savannah offers a perfect stop on the way to ports further north and for overland distribution to all points in the South. It's a match made in heaven, Governor."

This really perked him up. He clicked his fingers, jumped off his chair and, for a fraction of a second, I almost broke out in a little Tevya jig.

An aide was bending down and whispering in the Governor's ear. He looked at me with a smile wider than his face and revealed a set of healthy teeth and said, "I understand that you met Lieutenant Governor Maddox outside?"

"Yes, I did sir. It was a pleasure."

"I am sure it was."

We all left his office elated. The man had made an excellent impression. In subsequent visits I had with him, he could not have been more gracious. Discipline and efficiency emanated from him and his staff. It was clear why Jimmy Carter, an Annapolis graduate and engineer, had been picked by hard-driving Admiral Rickover, father of the US Navy's nuclear ships, to captain a nuclear submarine.

Later, I could not help observing that, as Governor, he surrounded himself with experts, consultants and advisers almost exclusively from New York, Boston, Philadelphia, Chicago and so on. Later, as President, however, he would be surrounded purely by Georgians.

At this point the whole thing needed a new wrapping. The name, the look, the logos – everything from the smallest thing, such as business cards, to the naming on the ships, the livery on the containers, all had to assume a universal image projecting the "new," efficiency, the state-of-the-art, in both the equipment and the service. I devised a brand new logo with a universal appeal. I looked at the forty-foot wide span of the containers as moving billboards and saw an ideal opportunity to get global exposure for the new service, in terms of both its name and size. An image supported by logos and sales slogans is effective if it is repeated consistently and in a uniform way. I observed that when traveling through cities, containers were viewable from high-rise offices, too. It would make sense to add identifying graphics on the roofs of the containers, impressing viewers from the top as well.

Since the ships were new, some people from the parent company felt compelled to propose names for them. They came up with names of old-line pioneering villages and historical landmarks - local names were not very applicable to the universally accepted use of the English language and the future of Savannah as a major port. I regarded the ships as part of the marketing and publicity; I strongly felt that the ships should all bear the names of the ports of call the line served. And that's how it went. From the Zim Hong Kong to the Zim Haifa, each of the six ships bore the name of a port of call. It demonstrated the scope of the company's reach in a constant, yet subtle way. Matching the flurry of expansion, the expected maiden arrival of the Zim Savannah in this very port kept everyone in a high state of excitement.

***

Back in New York, the PhD top honcho convened a brainstorming session, attended by key management. At issue was how to convert the loyal customers, whose loyalty was solely to pricing, to the new and modern ways of doing business, which now included investment in Savannah and a general reorganization. At the same time, there was the need to recruit hordes of new customers to this service. And not just once, but every time and with every nautical mile.

"How do you intend to do this?" I asked, regretting the question the minute it came out of my mouth.

"Simple. We shall double our sales, every time," came the answer from the PhD head honcho.

"How are you going to do it? Will you design an attractive product to go to market with? Will you establish a professional sales training program and then flood your markets with advertising, public relations, and attractive pricing in support?"

"You said it. Yes, that's it!" came back the reply, with a curved and satisfied smile. "But we need a slogan," he continued, "...and it must be a catchy sales slogan. It should run along the containers, so the whole world will see it."

"Do you have something in mind for such a slogan?"

"Of course. Here, Gideon, come over here for a minute. What was the slogan we coined the other day to boost sales?"

Gideon, a lanky, bald, bespectacled alumni of the Technion with a whole backpack full of degrees, rushed over from the window sill where he had answered a phone call in the middle of the meeting. He sat down and said:

"Ship it with Zim and forget it."

He accompanied this with both arms spread wide, his face a ball of tight concentration, and then finished off with a facial crescendo, an ear to ear smile, revealing a missing wisdom tooth.

Now everyone looked at me. My face was stone. The PhD, after a few more seconds, gave up on me, waved me off and started a conversation with the still excited Gideon.

"Are you serious!?" I screamed, "Of course you are. Do you know what you just said? Gideon, did you try to get booked for stand-up comedy?"

It took Gideon a few seconds to catch on and, as a designated executive in the new organization; this did not sit too well with him. I, for my part, realizing that this was what the meeting was all about, decided that this sloganeering had to stop.

"Your market is the import-export community. It is not retail sales to housewives. A jingle is not what you need. Have you formulated plans on how to fill your beautiful Strick boxes going back?" I decided to hit them in their soft underbellies. "You're not going to ship back empties? Are you?"

The meeting was over. When I left, I saw a bunch of them in lively, gesticulating discussions.

"There goes our slogan killer," they probably said.

***

Savannah is a lovely town. Graceful, full of Southern charm and a tinge of the weird. Terrific jazz in the dives down on the waterfront. The food should also be mentioned. It's American food, but not well-known to us Northerners. The place we loved and could not get back to often enough was Mrs. Wilkes' Dining Room on West Jones Street. Lunch is the time to indulge and man, do they let you. It's all round tables, seating ten. From eleven on there are long lines around the block and it's worth the wait. The food is brought to the table in heaps and one ladles out one's own portions. Baskets of breads and scones and you name it come along with it. One tastes a bit of heaven at Mrs. Wilkes' table. There is just one price and a very reasonable one at that, per person. Only thing is that you have to bring your empty plates - and boy were they empty - to the kitchen when finished. It is Southern cooking at its best.

Searching for accommodations near the port, I had walked through the beautifully laid-out twenty some-odd squares, each one different from the next, dissecting the historic district. Savannah used to be Georgia's capital; it was founded in the earlier part of the 18th century. Strolling along, I noticed a lovely little building next to one of the squares that advertised itself as a hotel. It was not too far from the river, so I moved into the neat, yet odd-shaped room that had a multi-faucet sink that ran along a portion of the wall. Chatting the next morning at coffee with the owner after a restful night, I found out that, not too long ago, this very building was one of Savannah's oldest funeral parlors, dating back to the beginning of the 19th century.

"We used to embalm in the room you slept in," he proudly informed me.

"So that's what that oversized sink was for. You did a wonderful job of making a hotel out of it," I complimented him.

Despite the convenience it offered and the lovely leafy square in front of it, I decided to leave my embalming room and crash in a real hotel with a history of the living.

Three forty-seven AM. The phone in my room rang in a very insistent manner. "I told them to wake me at 5:30, why are they waking me now?" I mumbled, half asleep.

"You with the Zim Savannah?"

"Yeah, what is it?"

"This is the Coast Guard station. You got problems. The ship got into a storm, two seamen are lost at sea, swept overboard, some containers, too, lost, dropped into the sea. Stay at this phone for updating."

"What!?" is all I could yell into the receiver. Then, collecting myself, I shouted, "No!"

"Yes," the Coast Guard man replied.

I rushed to put on my clothes and attempted to get a hold of the big PhD honcho. Couldn't get him. While I tried to reach him, I also tried to assemble the guys from last night in the lobby. I went through a quick list of all the calls I had to make. First, I called the local public relations firm to contact the Governor and, given the storm breaking all around me, to ask him to take a rain check. Within seconds, I got calls from the media; although I had nothing to tell them, this did not deter them from calling every few minutes. I tried to reach the company's operations center; they did not know what I was talking about. While all this was going on, I was trying to find out more and keep the line open for the Coast Guard, which was impossible. Somehow I wanted to believe that the Coast Guard would call me and say that it was all a false alarm. I was calling the Coast Guard every fifteen minutes. I ran to the bathroom to shave and looked in the mirror. 'Is this me? All this is happening to me? Now? And I am in the midst of this?' I wondered.

I kept thinking how to make the best of it. How can you, when people have lost their lives? What about their families? Have they been recovered? How do you handle this with the media? Well…first, stand up. Don't hide, don't invent, just tell the truth, all the way, as it plays out. Which we did.

It was a hectic day. Yet, the press queries relentlessly asked how we felt.

"Are you kidding? We feel bad, terrible, horrible, but our main concern is not the lost containers, it's the seamen and their families."

"How could this happen?" the media asked.

"It will be investigated, and then we'll have more details."

At the end of that day that never seemed to end, twenty-four hours later, I was asking myself whether I had signed up for this. The top honcho never got back to me. One of his gofers told me that he had just contracted the flu and was detained in New York. Nice.

Shortly before noon, our ship limped into port, accompanied by two Coast Guard vessels. Despite the rain, the press was there in force; it was the biggest news story that had happened in Savannah that day and during the ensuing week. Rows upon rows of television cameras were trained on the ship. We got more and more consistent coverage than we had bargained for. I held off any of the local publicity and public relations plans for another time. There was nothing we could add to it, as everything was delivered by the media a few times an hour. It dissipated a bit the following day and it took about a week until it quieted down. 'These would be the headlines till the next big news event,' I said to myself. And they were.

The Governor called, expressing great concern. He postponed his visit and the series of ceremonies, receptions, and interviews. We canceled appearances by the captain of the ship, who was mobbed by the media anyway. At the end, it was a maiden voyage, although a broken one. It never occurred again and Savannah remains an established port of call for the company's ships plying the Far East trade.

Oy!

I can't help comparing myself to my car. In terms of car-life my car is getting older. It is a 2007 model, an SUV and very good, or loyal as I call it. I would hate to change it, which is inevitable of course. It has relatively little mileage, a little over fifty thousand and I think the reason for it is that we have not driven up to Maine since we bought it. We used to go there two to three times a year.

The main reason for my comparison is medical of course. Well, the car gets maintained and whatever it needs, engine parts, lights, wipers, tires – you name it, you bring it in to Exxon Arnie who lately became Gulf Arnie and who within hours and with the aid of his very able deputies Kevin and Siresh, gets it all fixed, replaced, and done.

***

Now take me. Like everyone else I am gaining in years, but I have a lot more mileage than my car. When the knees go, you go to a specialist, then you go for a second opinion and then, if you really want to get confused, you go to a third one, "a really great one," the recommenda-tion pronounces. "He's doing some famous football players." Well, I've got a problem with that - my knees never played football, so maybe this guy is over-qualified or wants to build me up to be a football player.

I play tennis, or try to with the damaged knees. As you might notice, I do not call myself a tennis player, I will, though, as soon as I make it to the Open.

Then, it turns out that the hearing isn't so good. I need convincing because if people speak clearly and loudly I hear everything. "That's the typical sign of hearing loss," they tell me.

Really? I mull. But I only mull for a short time because the following week, when I go to my yearly eye checkup, the famous doctor tells me that I need cataract surgery and he's going to insert brand new sharp lenses behind the pupils. More mulling is in order now and I leave to go for lunch. I bite with vigor into my sandwich and before I know it, a crown I have and forgot about, lifts off and becomes part of the sand-wich. Off to the dentist who, after a reasonable amount of torture fixes it all beautifully. The moral of the story? – Don't order that kind of sandwich anymore.

***

Well this is what I envy my car for, you bring it in, ten different problems, mechanical, replacements, insertions, fluids, liquids, oils, and it's all done under one roof. In my case I've got to go under at least five roofs – the teeth, the ears, the eyes, the knees and, of course, the primary care doctor, the supervising producer of this whole shebang.

How come it all happens at the same time? Could it be age? I don't feel it, I feel like normal, until I am confronted by these experts. "Yes, normal," they agree, and then they put a tag line on it - "…for your age." Must be the accumulated mileage. That must be it, my car doesn't have much on it, so why am I trying to compare myself to it?

Oy

It's age, what else can it be? But let's be clear about it, I am not conceding to anything and will arm-wrestle with the best. But only with the left arm, the right one hurts all the time. Oy.

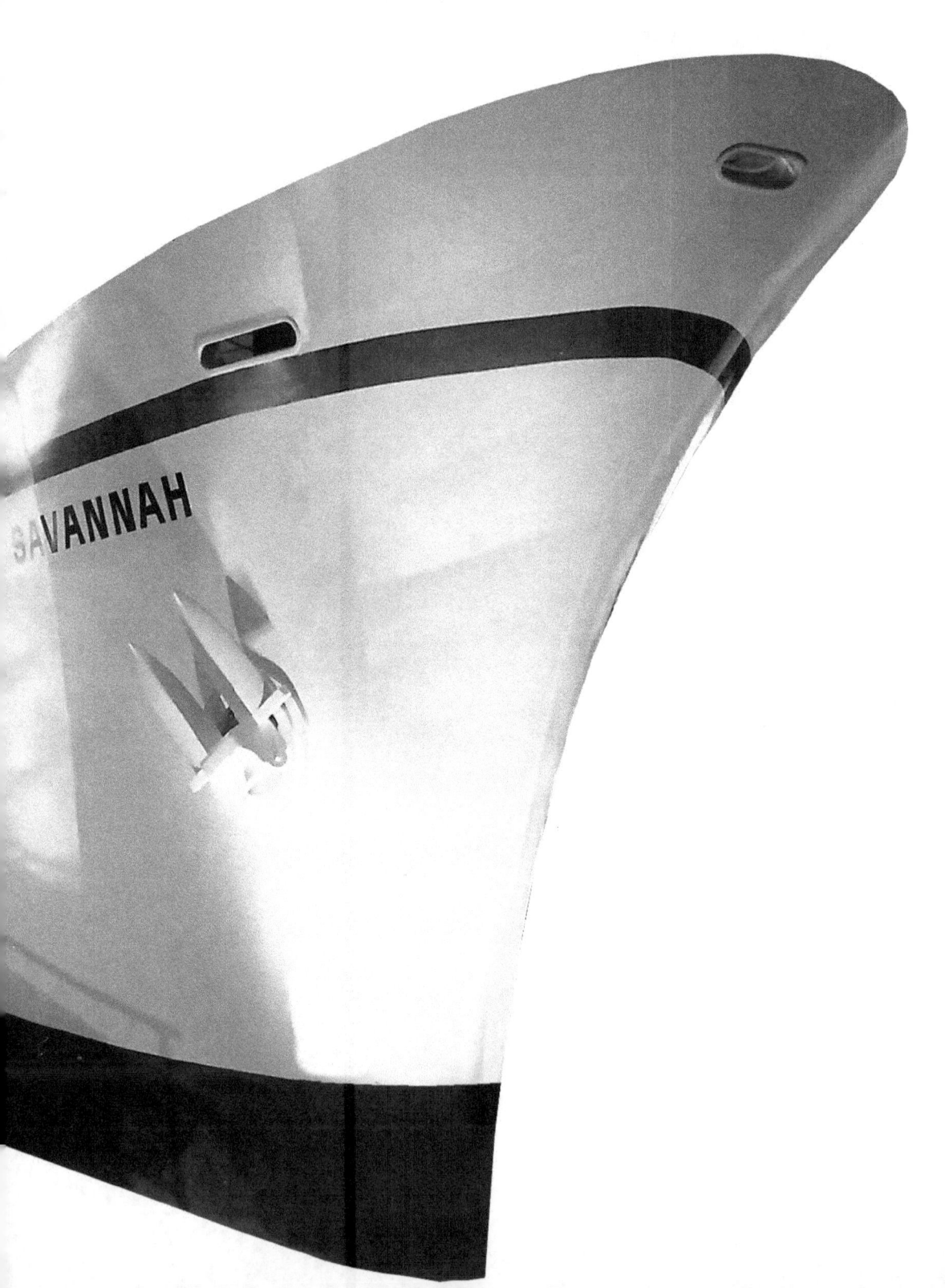

F. A. S. T. is Definitely Better

At the beginning of the sixties, the West Side piers of Manhattan were packed with ocean liners sporting a forest of colorful smoke stacks that represented their company and national colors. These ocean-going behemoths plied the Atlantic to Europe and on to Mediterranean ports and down through the Suez Canal to points even farther east. They were berthed right up to the street, disgorging and boarding their passengers. Overseas travel was mainly by ship, and the passenger piers were busy with traffic. Hulls were mostly black and white, ranging from the majestic Queens of the Cunard line, the Queen Elizabeth and Queen Mary to the Italian ships like the Cristoforo Colombo, the Leonardo daVinci and the Rafaelo and to others like the France, the Rotterdam, the Amsterdam and many more.

Yet, the star of this array was the latest, most advanced and stream-lined SS United States, the brand new pride of the US Lines, and the record holder for the fastest ship crossing the big pond. There were other great American ships as well, like the Independence and the Constitution of American Export Lines, servicing a string of Mediterranean ports. This was before container ships took over the freight transportation business and the airlines siphoned off the passengers from the piers. The piers, after a period of idleness, morphed into sports venues and some were kept for the occasional cruise ship that happened along and for the annual visiting Naval flotillas on the 4th of July. The carrier Intrepid found a permanent home on one of the former passenger piers and was turned into a naval air museum.

Many of these shipping lines were clients of our exhibition and design company, assigning to us special projects and the design of exhibitions they needed for trade show events and international travel conferences. One of our earlier clients was American Export Lines. They had a series of cargo and passenger ships but the stars were the SS Independence and the SS Constitution luxury liners, bearing patriotic names after the originals berthed in Boston harbor. An extensive fleet of cargo ships roamed the seas, bulk carriers and freighters that called on every port across the globe and carried the well-recognized company flag with its big E embedded in a diamond on a red field.

In charge of the company was Jacob Isbrandtsen, a scion of a prominent Danish ship-owning family, going back generations. Jakob Isbrandtsen knew the business he was born into. He had a few pronounced dislikes, foremost amongst them the mountains of red tape he had to struggle with in the course of his business. He also had a dislike for certain minorities and was the owner of a short fuse. One day, as we discussed themes that would promote future exhibition projects and possible "showstoppers," he suddenly went to the pen, where employees toiled at their desks, lifted sheaves of paper off their desks and went to the display window fronting Broadway at Battery Park. He opened the window space from the inside and dumped the pile of documents in the window. Then he wrote with a heavy black marker on a white piece of paper: "This is the paperwork required to ship one ton of freight on an American ship!!!" He crowned it with three successive exclamation marks and then he stormed outside to admire his handiwork from street level, and engaging in conversation with passers-by who stopped to admire the display. He felt markedly better, the steam was let out and the rage having dissipated left him. There were half a dozen street level display windows that drew spectators during lunchtime when people were lolling outside on sunny days and Jacob Isbrandtsen chose this venue for his protests. The Isbrandtsen Steamship Lines had bought American Export and it became known as American Export Isbrandtsen Lines.

I was introduced to Jakob Isbrandtsen by Charlie Lundgren, a known marine painter, who painted portraits of yachts belonging to shipping owners and wealthy members of the New York Yacht Club, who then hung these oils in their offices, boardrooms and in the New York Yacht Club. Charlie was a yachtsman in his own right too and had participated in a few Bermuda races. His very lovely and talented daughter, a gifted artist, worked in our design and art department. One thing stood out in those early sixties, although New York was brimming with Jews, you could not find one in that whole environment.

I was summoned to a meeting one day and was introduced to Admiral Will, a war-time naval commander who had directed the submarine forces of the Seventh Fleet at the battles of Midway and Guam in WWII. The admiral, now retired, was the chairman of American Export Isbrandtsen Lines and took a special interest in a newly formed subsidiary company that would operate the first nuclear powered merchant ship. The task was assigned to the company by the government, who owned the ship, the NS Savannah.

The admiral was a gentleman's gentleman. Silver haired, tall and of erect bearing, clear-voiced and with piercing eyes that looked at one straight on. You could tell that he took your measure without losing a detail.

"Gentlemen," he addressed the gathering of advertising people, newly assigned staff, executives from other divisions and my humble self. "The new company will be known as First Atomic Rapid Transport. It defines our mission. We need to convey an image of this historical undertaking, a very first ever atomic energy powered commercial ship that will sail the seas. It is a revolutionary task, a landmark departure from steam and traditional fuels. The purpose of this company is to operate the Nuclear Ship Savannah for the United States government and our country." With that he slammed the flat of his hand on his desk.

While I listened to him, I scribbled the name down on my pad. I was conjuring up all sorts of possible graphic images in my head. I sifted it down to its acronym, which I knew was going to be the way it would be used. It was always the case and if you did not offer an acronym, people would make it up themselves. I was looking and checking my scribblings again and again and I couldn't believe what I was looking at.

I raised my arm, "Admiral sir, you cannot use the name, no way." The surprised admiral, as well as the assembled crowd around in the room, looked up surprisingly with all eyes on me. The admiral's face was becoming perturbed and bemused at the same time.

Being the polite Virginia gentleman he was, he looked at me and asked, "And may I inquire as to the nature of your objection that should prevent me from pursuing the name?"

"Sir, the company will be known by its acronym. So please sir, just read the acronym."

He now spelled it out on his pad FART. He looked up again, looked at me and conceded while a wave of chuckling murmurs engulfed the room.

"Thank you. We better not. Cross the whole thing off."

"Sir, it is not all bad, we don't have to discard the idea, How's this: First Atomic Ship Transport. We just change a letter, we throw out the R and replace with an S. FAST is a good name and it reflects what we do, sir."

"Indeed, absolutely, I couldn't have said it better, I like FAST. Gentlemen, FAST has beaten FART; adjust your targets now."

After everyone had left, he put his hand on my shoulder and said, "Thank you. If I still had a ship, I'd want you on it."

"Admiral Sir, if I would enlist I would only do so under your command," I replied.

Two weeks later we met again. He sat behind this huge desk that stood at an angle to the room. Every time I was in his office I imagined the front panel dropping down any minute and the cannons coming out, waiting for the Admiral's command to fire.

"We are going to the World's Fair in Flushing Meadows," he said. "We need a special exhibit, featuring the Savannah. Westinghouse is giving us an actual model of the nuclear machinery, and we can have people walk through the ship and view the atomic powered engines."

And that's what we did. I designed this whole gigantic thing. I loved this project. We built a replica of the streamlined hull. Visitors could enter the ship through a gang plank, view the nuclear engines and exit on the opposite side after going through the ship. It worked and looked great and it was gratifying to see people lining up, waiting to board despite that we had no give-aways, no Belgian Waffles, no Wisconsin cheeses, nothing but viewing a historical first, and an atomic ship engine.

At the end, FAST prevailed and FART retreated quietly, without a sound.

I started thinking, what's this with me and Savannah? Somehow, years later, I met up with Savannah again, this time the City of Savannah and a container ship I named Savannah, all on another and different maritime assignment. Life's coincidences, I guess.

Moments

Shanghai

I was sitting in the back of a cab, crawling to the airport. We were on Nanjing Road in Shanghai, in the midst of a perpetual hustle and bustle that makes one admire the fact that, in the midst of this mayhem anything moved at all.

Nanjing Road is a main drag stretching from the edge of the Huangpu River and the Bund all the way to the airport, dissecting downtown. The street is narrow and tree-lined and today a crew was out trimming the trees on both sides of the street. They were armed with hand saws, ladders and ropes. Some of the workers were ensconced in the trees, swinging from limbs while sawing off branches that came crashing down with complete disregard as to who or what they might hit. And hit they did - cars, people, horse-drawn carts, cyclists, and everything below the roadway and sidewalk. Screams and threats erupted and fists waved in the air every time a crash occurred. Yet, the crews in the trees were heedless as to what went on below them, deaf to the protests. So tree limbs and branches kept on raining down. Connoisseurs of this scene were ardently watching their movements and as soon as a limb was about to be sawn through, the bets were placed as to who and what was going to get it next when that branch came crashing down. Drivers stuck their hands out, clutching money bills eager to participate in this street roulette, managed by a croupier who sprang up from nowhere, busily dashing between the cars. Money could be made even on a slow speed, high-volume traffic day.

Having finally passed this obstacle, another detour/delay was up ahead, forcing cars to funnel into one lane to circumvent a stalled car. A man emerged from that car, shrugging his shoulders, smiling sheepishly and gesticulating his helplessness by pointing to the stalled car. He resolutely opened his trunk, took out a rope, fastened it to the front of the car, securing it to what looked like the front axle and started pulling it. Some passersby came to his assistance and pushed it from the rear and the sides and in minutes removed the obstacle from the road and onto the sidewalk where the car came to rest. It was impressive to observe the self-reliance and practical determination of this driver.

A couple of months later I was on the way to an airport again, this time in Moscow. We were on a highway and moved swiftly. On the side of the road was a disabled car, all its doors and trunk were gapingly open. On the floor of the car sat a man, observing the traffic flow that passed him by, smiling sheepishly. He had taken off his jacket, waving to us with one hand while holding a bottle of Vodka in the other, from which he sipped from time to time, waiting to be rescued. In the meantime, he worked at making himself as comfortable as possible.

For me it was déjà vu. What was striking of course were the two pictures. The Chinese man just took matters in his hands, tied a rope to the car and pulled it. The Russian sat there reconciling himself to his fate that morning, resorting to his vodka and, with an expression of "What is there to do?" he succumbed, not too unhappily, to his situation.

Is this an indicator of something - a study of national character, or just nothing? Good thing I am not an academic. An in-depth, extended scientific opinion might have resulted.

Tehran

The concierge at the Intercontinental Hotel motioned to me and told me that a fellow had responded to the little notice I had posted on his counter looking for a tennis partner. I had taken on this habit of posting these notices whenever I checked into a hotel on business. I welcomed the exercise and could always use a break from attending meetings and sitting all day in conferences.

"There he sits!" The well-greased concierge pointed to a cluster of chairs in the center of the lobby. Indeed, a local twenty-something fellow with a tennis racquet leaning against his chair sat there. We met and were ready to play. I rushed to my room to change and we were on our way to the courts, located behind the hotel.

I opened a brand new can of balls I had brought with me from the States and hit a practice ball over to him. He missed it, picked up the ball and placed it in his pocket. I hit the second ball trying to start a rally with him. This one, too, he missed and stashed it in his pocket. I hit the third ball over - again he missed it and pocketed it as well. He then turned suddenly and took off towards Elizabeth Avenue, mixed with the crowd and disappeared from sight.

This was the strangest tennis encounter I had ever had. Later, when I found out that a can of three American balls goes for twenty bucks and up, it did not look so strange anymore.

Harbin

After a short time in Harbin, the northernmost major city in China, bordering Siberia, I noticed the smooth, even streets, unlike the pothole-rutted streets in other cities. They were perfect and seemed well-tended. At the first opportunity I commented on this phenomenon.

"It is very simple," my hostess explained, "…it is February now and we have a foot of ice on the road, very smooth, looks nice."

"No chains, no salt?" I kept on.

"No, no, we do not like chains and salt damages the cars."

"No accidents?" I wondered.

"No, did you see any?"

"None," I had to admit. It was very cold, colder than cold. Interestingly it brought out the ladies' fashions. Many active ladies in business were dressed to the hilt and stood out. Life revolved around the indoors. A residue and remnant of European culture and habits was evident, with lots of very wet dinner parties lasting until the wee hours.

The Germans had started the beer industry there and vodka and champagne were ever-present, too. A good thing. It warmed and it enlivened the inside where most of the people congregated, except when visiting the marvelous ice sculpture competition in the park. It was also one of the rare Chinese cities where one would see blondes. Harbin, from the days of the Czars, drew Europeans, Russians, Germans and European Jews who had escaped Hitler during the war years.

Back to the smoothest streets, the ice pavement one could call it. It was amazing to watch drivers, driving in a normal fashion, all without any wintry equipment as if the road was a new shiny concrete one.

Minneapolis

We were late arrivals in Minneapolis, where a fellow from my office and I had come for a three day business agenda. A taxi at the airport took us to a hotel, whose name escapes me now. It was past nine in the evening and we were proceeding in the wintry darkness along snow-covered streets. In a section that looked rather quiet, the taxi made a U-turn in the middle of the street, pulled up and dropped us off in front of a red brick structure with imposing arches, large windows and even a few gargoyles here and there, and then was gone.

"Well, let's go inside and see what goes on here."

Our agent had booked this place and he was usually very good in his choices. So far, at least. We lifted our luggage and presentation cases and opened the heavy oak door, presumably to our hotel. In the cold and in our anxiety to get into a warm interior, we did not pay attention to the lack of any signage and lights. As we stepped in, we stepped out. We had just walked through a facade, the kind Hollywood does with film sets; there was nothing behind it, except for an empty, garbage-strewn lot.

"Welcome to Minneapolis!" We congratulated each other while bending over in cramps of laughter and stepping back out through the door and dragging our luggage back to the street.

"Not even a doorman to help with the luggage," we complained to no one.

All this was before cell phones and no pay phone was to be found anywhere in the vicinity. Traffic was sparse until finally, a forlorn cab came along.

"What are you guys doing here? You look like normal people."

"Maybe YOU can tell us. That's what we were trying to figure out. Where are we, what is here? Get us to Minneapolis please."

In Minneapolis proper, we still tried to figure out what had gone through the mind of the airport taxi when he dropped us off in front of what was once a hotel's remaining facade.

"But we have to admit, judging from the facade, this must have been some hotel."

"It's simple," I concluded. "We were a late arrival - a few years too late."

Dalian

Dalian is an important port city in China's north. In the thirties, when the Japanese attacked China, it was their port of entry into Mongolia. Remnants of their rule, mostly former government buildings, can still be seen in Dalian. Some have large outdoor billboards tacked on to them, sponsored by the local Cadillac dealer. It is an aggressive, developing city with a large Industrial Development Zone housing many international companies.

We were discussing the establishment of a panel manufacturing facility investment in the Development Zone, with my Italian friends, the owners of this specialized construction technology and the local Dalian partner. We were about a dozen people around the table, talking, translating, and many munching on the generous hospitality of our Dalian hosts, who heaped up little baskets of oranges, piles of peanuts, bananas, and water bottles, hardly leaving room on the table for the voluminous stacks of paper.

As the review of the legal documents commenced, a nice fellow from Dalian, an English-speaking lawyer representing the local partner, repeatedly jumped up, calling out "No!" every time we arrived at a new paragraph.

I had befriended this fellow the day before, who insisted on being called Fred. This was a pretty convenient request, because the proper pronunciation of the Chinese names proved difficult sometimes, especially when there was more than one of the same name present.

Thus after the fourth interruption by Fred, which led to delays and slowed down the whole process, I asked him to step outside for a smoke.

He was gushing all over, a friendly happy individual. I offered him a cigar and we lit up.

"Now Freddy, my friend, what's gotten into you? You are doing gymnastics, jumping up from your chair and yelling "No!" every time we get to a new paragraph or debate a section. You are the lawyer, you supposed to help, be constructive, make sure this deal works."

Now Freddy was enamored with everything American. He carefully checked out how we were dressed, how we talked, how we walked. His English was above the passable and when he did not jump up, he was helpful.

"Well, let me tell you, I do like American lawyers," he confessed.

"Like American lawyers?"

"Yes, yes, they always jump up and cry "No!" I've seen it many times."

"Freddy, you may have looked at the wrong lawyers. Please forget them."

"But they looked so American."

Eilat

I love the desert, especially when it is on the shores of a fabulous sea that holds a collection of the most exotic tropical fish in a bewildering array of colors and is the world's second largest coral collection after the Barrier Reef in Australia. We checked into a hotel for our fortnight vacation stay.

Soon we stood on our terrace and absorbed the view and what a view it was. We had been facing the mountain range in Saudi Arabia on one side and the jagged mountains of the Sinai Peninsula on the other side. The shimmering waters of the Gulf of Aqabah were lapping at the shore, which ran along four countries, Egypt, Israel, Jordan, and Saudi Arabia on the far end. We were absorbed with the view when we were suddenly interrupted by an insistent knock on the door.

As I opened the door, a fellow in paint-splattered overalls carrying a bucket of paint and a ladder made his way into the room and cheerfully announced that he came to paint the walls.

"You will like it!" he assured us, staring at our astonished faces. "I hope you do not mind," he said. "I am a little late."

"It's about time," I blurted out, smiling. "No, of course we do not mind, why would we? We only just checked in and were about to unpack, change clothes and go down to the beach, so please go ahead."

Eilat at that time was in the throes of development and new hotels seemed to spring up.

"Now this is service. Hotels change the linen for new guests coming in, so why not repaint the walls? Pretty good idea, nice touch of service," I said to my wife.

We sat on the edge of the bed, watching him paint. When he was done he stepped back, evaluating his work with a professional eye, almost landing on the edge of the bed we sat on. He then went to the other corner of the room, tilted his head, checked further, nodded his head, threw us a look, smiled and said, "Good!"

We applauded, he bowed and he bid us "Goodbye" banging his ladder on part of the newly painted wall and left. Now how many hotels provide this kind of service while the guests are in the room? Not many, I bet.

Kibbutz Business

Sometime in the 1960's on a trip to Israel I saw a set of beautiful plastic tiles, imprinted with images of the Bible's Flora and Fauna. They were exquisitely executed and were truly outstanding. I decided to buy a few sets as giveaways. Back home, the tiles met with unusual success and organizations asked me to get a shipment for them. A distributor in the field with a large client base wanted to introduce these tiles to his line of goods and asked me to assist with this the next time I should happen to be in Israel.

On my next trip to Israel I went back to the Kibbutz that produced these tiles to see whether they had the capacity to take an order of ten thousand and deliver it on time. The manager of the factory said that he could do it, that they could reproduce all twenty-four images of the Flora and Fauna and, with enough advance notice, would deliver on time by bringing the load to El Al or to a ship in Haifa for transport.

Okay so far, I figured, so now we came to the cost. My friend asked me to get an idea of the price structure. All I knew about cost was what I paid for them when I bought them in a store, which was somewhere in the neighborhood of six dollars and fifty cents each, including a piece of felt in the back and a picture hook.

The factory manager had a tortured look on his face, battling to arrive at his final sales price.

"Well, I think we got it," he finally said to me in semi-relief as we sat outside, under a tree, at a picnic table spooning yogurt, "…it'll be ten dollars and seventy-six cents a tile."

"What?" I cried out and almost lost my balance and was close to falling off my chair. I paid six dollars and fifty cents for a single tile, so how can ten thousand cost more per piece?"

"Of course they cost more," a big frown was collecting over his forehead as he answered. "It is more work!"

"That is true." I tried to put him at ease, but decided not to expound on the production system of volume, cost efficiencies and a few other things. Socialism met capitalism and I wanted the twain to meet? Well, reality is not a uniform thing, it does not fit all.

The tiles were never ordered and a pity it was, as they were really exquisite.

Madrid

Spending a few days in Madrid on vacation, my wife and I decided to attend a bull fight. Although we were not aficionados, we decided not to leave Madrid without seeing one.

We approached our hotel concierge, who secured the tickets for us, chose a particular "very, very good" matador and a bull from a famous hacienda in Burgos. The concierge prided himself on his English and we had frequent conversations with him.

The weather, although sunny and warm for the past few days, turned cloudy and the sun played hide and seek, intermittently appearing and disappearing behind the clouds.

We got to the arena and, at the given time, the colorful ceremonies started and the bulls were led into the arena. The program offered different matadors, toreadors, picadors and all kinds of Isidors who appeared and performed to the cheers and boos of the very participatory crowd. Then, suddenly, the skies turned dark and the arena's lights went on as it became darker yet. It looked ominous. As the matador was about to give the bull the coup-de-grace, sudden loud rumblings and terrible-sounding claps of thunder galloped through the arena and the sky opened up, releasing a torrent of water that made one feel as if one was standing under Niagara Falls. People scattered, jumped over seats and stampeded in all directions to the exits. And we joined the flight.

When we arrived back at the hotel, soaked to the bone and dripping puddles on the lobby floor, the news of the arena debacle was already spread all over. Our loyal concierge came out with towels. He put on his best hotel-English and wanted to know details.

"So check out time? Everybody check out?"

"Yes," we confirmed to his wonderment, "...yes, everybody checked out, the bulls too."

"So sorry for you," he added.

"No matter, we loved the whole thing." We really did.

Xian

Xian is endowed with historical riches. It is a jewel box. It's the place, since 210 BC, where the spectacular life size terracotta warrior army protecting the tomb of China's first Emperor, Qin Shih Huang in his afterlife. It is one of the oldest cities in the world, over seven thousand years old. It is replete with royal tombs and as yet uncovered archeological treasures all around it. Throughout the city are the magnificent Bell and Drum Towers and the Big and Little Goose Pagodas. It was one of the ancient Chinese capitals as well as the starting point of the fabulous Silk Road.

The local Holiday-Inn featured two restaurants, each with its own menu. One was billed as a Western style restaurant and the other as a local Chinese one, of course. The Western restaurant was supposed to carry and serve Western-style food products, such as sandwiches, according to the menu. One day during my stay there, I settled down in the Western restaurant for lunch and ordered a ham and cheese sandwich.

"Just plain, ham and cheese, OK?" I was looking for assurances from the waiter.

"Yes, yes," he said and was gone.

About twenty-five minutes later, I saw my waiter, balancing a plate high above his head, progressing towards my table. I noticed smoke coming out of whatever he carried on the plate.

"Your sandwich, Mister," the waiter announced with a flourish and proudly placed the plate in front of me, stepped back, looked at me waiting for confirmation that indeed he brought a sandwich.

"This is the sandwich?" I timidly asked the frowning waiter.

"Yes, yes - sandwich!"

It looked like an accident had befallen it. It was soggy, and eating it one would need a spoon. Smoke was emanating from its center - it was like a miniature replica of an erupting Vesuvius.

"Why did you steam it? I asked for plain, just the ham and cheese," I admonished him.

"You eat sandwich cold? Just like that, cold?"

"Yes, I do, can I get one cold?"

"I do not know. I better ask kitchen."

"Good idea."

A culture clash over a sandwich was brewing. The kitchen, too, could not conceive of how a person, not lost in a jungle and living among wild animals, could eat a sandwich cold. It started with the bread, something that's not on the Chinese food menu. It certainly looked like it needed a bit of cooking up. So the least one could do to it, to mitigate its rawness, was steam it. And that's what they did and that's what was meant by a sandwich on the menu.

About the Author

Photo by Victoria Kaufman

Alex Kaufman lives and works in New York. He is a writer and his daily blog SAL & AL - Opinions from the Trenches covers any subject of human endeavor that passes us daily - in politics, sports, business, art, nationally and internationally, clearing obfuscations and double-talk and calling it as he sees it. He is happiest when he has more than four balls in the air and it's got to be interesting. Aside from writing, he keeps collecting experiences in business, in museum design, in travel and research for his next book and best of all, interaction with his grand-daughter, Victoria. He is the recent author of *The Precipice Option*, of *Trawling Twenty Centuries* and *On the Road to Halicz*.

To reach the author: author@timeflies-book.com

Time Flies is available at:
Amazon.com, BarnesandNoble.com, www.timeflies-book.com

Books by Alex Kaufman

Time Flies
www.timeflies-book.com

The Precipice Option
www.the-precipice-option.com

Trawling Twenty Centuries
www.trawlinghistory.com

Sal and Al/Opinions from the Trenches
www.salandal-thebook.com

On the Road to Halicz
www.roadtohalicz.com

Doodles
www.doodles-book.com

XELA Artbooks
www.xelaart.com

www.ingramcontent.com/pod-product-compliance
Lightning Source LLC
Chambersburg PA
CBHW080733250626
47170CB00010B/2818